RACHEL GRANT

WITHHOLDING EVIDENCE

JANUS PUBLISHING, LLC

This one is for Naomi

For showing me unconditional big-sister love for as long as I can remember.

CHAPTER ONE

Falls Church, Virginia
August

TRINA SORENSEN STIFFENED her spine and rang the town house doorbell. She couldn't hear a chime, so after a moment of hesitation, she followed up with a knock. Seconds ticked by without any sound of movement on the other side. She rang the bell again, and then repeated the knock for good measure. The front door was on the ground floor, next to the garage. Glancing upward, she checked out the windows of the two upper floors. No lights on, but at nine in the morning on a hot August day in Falls Church, that didn't tell her anything. If the man she hoped to meet was home, he'd have to descend at least one flight of stairs, possibly two.

Patience.

She was about to ring the bell again when the door whipped open, startling her. She stepped back, then remembered she needed to project poise and straightened to meet her target's gaze.

Keith Hatcher was even more handsome in person than in his official Navy photo, but she couldn't let that fluster her. It just meant he'd been blessed with good genes, a rather superficial measure of a person, really.

She took a deep breath and held out her hand. "Mr. Hatcher, Trina Sorensen, historian with Naval History and Heritage Command. I'd like to ask you a few questions about Somalia." She cringed as she said the last part. Too perky. Too eager. That was *not* how to approach a former Navy SEAL when asking about a mission.

Sporting tousled dark hair that suggested he may have just gotten out of bed, and wearing low-rise jeans and nothing else, the man leaned an impressive bare bicep against the doorframe and raised a quizzical thick eyebrow. "Trina? Cute name." He smiled.

"It fits." He reached out and touched the top of her head. "But I think you should go back to the day care center you escaped from and leave me alone." He stepped back, and the door slammed shut.

She jolted back a step. He did *not* just pat her on the head and slam the door in her face.

Except that was exactly what Senior Chief Petty Officer Keith Hatcher had done.

She was aware she looked young, but dammit, she was thirty-one freaking years old—the same age as Hatcher. In fact, she was a few weeks *older* than him. She squared her shoulders and rang the bell again.

Seconds ticked by. Then minutes. She pounded with the side of her fist.

Finally the door opened. "Yes?" He leaned against the doorjamb again, this time stretching out an arm to touch the hinged side of the opening. His body language conveyed amusement mixed with annoyance.

"Senior Chief, I'm *Dr. Trina Sorensen*"—she never referred to herself with the pretentious title of doctor, but figured his crack about day care warranted it—"and I'm researching your SEAL team's work in Somalia five years ago for Naval History and Heritage Command and the Pentagon. You must answer my questions."

"Dollface, it's Sunday morning. The only thing I *must* do today is jack off."

She crossed her arms. "Fine. I can wait. It'll be what, one, maybe two minutes?"

The man tilted his head back and laughed. She saw her opportunity and ducked under his arm, entering, as she'd suspected, an enclosed staircase. The door to the left could only go to the garage. She went straight for the stairs, heading up to his home. Her heart beat rapidly at her own audacity, but she was never going to get the information she needed to do her job from the SEAL without taking risks.

"What the hell?" he sputtered, then added, "Who do you think you are, barging into my home?"

"I told you. I'm Dr. Trina Sorensen from NHHC," she answered as she reached the landing that ended in the most spotless mudroom she'd ever seen. She crossed the room and stepped into his kitchen. Equally spotless. Either he had an amazing cleaning service, or he was a total neat freak. Given his disheveled appearance, she'd expected a disheveled home.

She leaned against a counter as he paused in his own kitchen doorway. His mouth twitched, but his jaw was firm, making her think he couldn't decide if he was annoyed or amused.

"I'll wait here while you masturbate. We can start the interview when you're done."

Amusement won, and a corner of his mouth kicked up. He took a step toward her. "It'll go faster if you help me."

Her heart thumped in a slow, heavy beat. Barging into his home might've been a mistake. She frowned. *Of course it was a mistake.* "I'm good to go. Already took care of business this morning in the shower. You go ahead without me."

He barked a sharp laugh, then shook his head. "What do you want, Dr. Sorensen?"

"As I said already, I'm here to ask you questions about Somalia." She pulled her digital recorder from her satchel. "Do you mind if I record our conversation?"

His brown eyes narrowed. "Hell, yes, I mind. More importantly, we aren't having a conversation. You are leaving. Now. Before I call the police."

"Please don't be difficult. I'm just doing my job."

"SEAL ops are classified." All hint of amusement left his voice, leaving only hard edges.

She sighed in frustration. Hadn't he bothered to read any of her e-mails? "I sent you what you need to verify my security clearance in my e-mail. And my orders came directly from the Pentagon."

"I don't give a crap if the pope sent you on orders from the president. I'm not telling you shit about a place I've never been."

He expected her to accept that and walk away? She'd never have gotten anywhere as a military historian if she allowed the men in her field to brush her off. "Oh, you've been to Somalia all right. You were there on a reconnaissance mission, gathering data about a rising al Qaeda leader who was taking advantage of a power vacuum created by ongoing interclan violence."

He crossed his arms and spoke softly. "I have no clue what you're talking about."

The man had a solid poker face; no hint that she'd surprised

him with the paltry facts she knew. So he was handsome and big
and had the most gorgeous sculpted pecs and abs she'd ever seen,
and he was sharp to boot. "I'm researching various SEAL actions
in Somalia over the last two decades, starting with Operation
Gothic Serpent and ending with yours."

He cocked his head. "Who is your boss?"

"Mara Garrett, interim director of the history department at
Naval History and Heritage Command."

His eyes widened when she said her boss's name. At last, a
break in the poker face. Did he recognize Mara's name from her
trouble in North Korea, her notorious run-in with Raptor, or
because he knew Mara was married to the US Attorney General?
Regardless, the name Mara Garrett opened doors, and Trina had
one more threshold she wanted to traverse—from the kitchen to
the living room, where she could conduct a proper interview.

"The work I did when I was in the Navy is classified. Not only
do I not have to tell you about an op I was never on in a country
I've never visited, but I could also get in serious trouble if I *did* tell
you a damn thing about the places I *have* been."

She handed him her card. "But you do have to answer me. The
Pentagon wants this report. Your input is necessary." This project
was her big break. Future naval operations could depend on her
findings, and the biggest of the brass were eager for this account.
She was already having visions of moving out of the cubicle next
to cantankerous Walt. She could have walls. And a door.

"But, you see there, dollface, that's the problem. I'm not in the
Navy anymore. I don't take orders from the Pentagon. I don't
have to follow commands from anyone, least of all a five-foot-
nothing librarian who invaded my kitchen without my
permission."

She straightened her spine and threw back her shoulders,
determined to reach her full height. "I'm five foot three. And I'm
an historian." Her glasses slipped, and she nudged them back to
the bridge of her nose.

He chuckled, and she flushed. She'd have been better off if she
hadn't corrected him on the librarian label as she adjusted her
glasses.

"Whatever, doll. Listen, you have one minute to get out of my
house, or I'm going to assume you've decided to watch me jerk off
after all."

She couldn't look away from the brown eyes that held hers in a tense gaze. Just her luck that he was so frigging gorgeous. Attractive men made her self-conscious. Especially ripped, half-naked ones. "I'm not playing games, Senior Chief. I'm just here to do my job."

He smiled slowly and reached for his fly.

Ψ

KEITH LAUGHED AS the woman bolted down the stairs and out of his town house. He was sort of sorry to see her go, because that exchange had been fun—certainly worth getting out of bed for.

He waited until he heard the front door slam, then followed and locked the door. What kind of fool showed up at a guy's house at nine on a Sunday morning and expected him to be forthcoming about an op that was not only top secret but was also the single greatest and worst moment of his military career? As if he'd tell her—or anyone—about Somalia.

He'd been debriefed after the op. The people who needed to know what happened knew everything. It was enough for the powers that be, and it was enough for him.

He climbed the stairs and returned to his kitchen, where he made a pot of coffee. The woman—Trina—had been hot in a sexy, nerdy-librarian sort of way. There was probably a fancy name for the way she wore her hair in that twist at her nape, but to him it was a bun. And the little glasses with the red rims? Sexy as hell the way they slanted over her hazel eyes.

Did she dress the part of librarian on purpose, or was it some sort of weird requirement of her profession? It was too bad she hadn't decided to stay, because he had a hard-on after watching her march up his stairs in that straight skirt that cradled her ass.

He'd always had a thing for librarians—or historians—whatever.

If she had a PhD, she was probably a lot older than she looked. *Thank goodness.* Of course, she could be some sort of Doogie Howser genius.

Mug of coffee in hand, he headed into his office, woke his computer, and clicked on the mail icon. Had she really e-mailed him? It seemed like he'd have noticed.

New e-mail notifications came pouring in. Shit. How long had it been since he loaded e-mail? He checked the date of the first ones—from his dad, of course. These were nearly two weeks old. Oh yeah, he'd been so upset after the last round of antigovernment, antimilitary e-mails from his dear old dad, he'd turned off the mail program and took it out of start-up so it wouldn't run unless he initiated it. For some reason that had felt easier, less final, than blocking his father's e-mail address.

Thanks to the constant barrage of ranting messages, three months ago Keith had set his phone to only load e-mails from a select number of approved addresses. In the last two weeks, since he shut off mail on the computer, he'd received e-mails from the people who mattered to him on his phone, allowing him to forget he wasn't receiving everything on the computer.

He scanned the list, deleting the ones from his dad without opening any. Each time he tapped the button, he felt a twinge of guilt. It was time to block Dad once and for all. Yet he still refused to take that final step and wasn't quite sure why.

Misguided hope the man would change, he supposed.

After he'd deleted several e-mails, the name Trina Sorensen popped to the top of the list—the time stamp was last night. He scrolled down further and found four e-mails from her in the last week.

He opened her most recent message, noting the return address was indeed official Navy. He scanned the contents. Huh. She'd told him that since he hadn't responded to her previous inquiries, she would be stopping by his house this morning, and if he didn't want her to show up, he should reply.

He lifted a finger to hit the Delete button and paused. Dammit. He owed her an apology.

Then he smiled, remembering that tight ass and those sexy calves. He'd liked the way she was quick with a comeback and didn't back down easily.

He wouldn't apologize via e-mail. He wanted talk to her in person so he could see her again. No way was he going to tell her about Somalia, but he could explain that in person too. Sort of.

Maybe his interest in the historian was only because he was bored. But at least she'd given him a reason to get out of bed this morning. Unemployment was for shit. He needed to *do* something.

An e-mail from his buddy Alec Ravissant reminded him of the garden party this afternoon at the home of Dr. Patrick Hill, the head of The MacLeod-Hill Exploration Institute in Annapolis,

Maryland. Rav was running for the open Senate seat in Maryland, and the party was intended to introduce Rav to Hill's extensive connections in local politics and the military.

Hill's guests would be power-hungry high-society and military personnel. People who wanted to ingratiate themselves with military leaders, like the socialite made infamous in the Petraeus scandal a while back.

Sorry, Rav. No way in hell. Keith might be bored in his very early retirement, but he wasn't bored enough to attend a party that would require fending off the advances of married women while their husbands stood idly by, either oblivious, uncaring, or hoping their wives' infidelity would gain them admission into the centers of power.

Christ. He was starting to sound like his dad.

Just before he hit the Delete button, his eye caught the note at the bottom. Curt Dominick would be there, and Rav wanted to introduce them. Keith knew the US Attorney General had been the one to finally convince Rav to run for the Senate, so it was no surprise that Dominick would attend. He was both a power player and a good friend of Rav's. What gave Keith pause was realizing the man's wife, Mara Garrett—who happened to be sexy Trina the historian's boss—would probably attend as well.

Something Rav had said rang a bell—didn't the MacLeod-Hill Institute have some sort of oceanic-mapping joint venture with the Navy? Specifically with the Navy's underwater archaeology branch?

A quick Google search answered that question—yes—and revealed that the Navy's underwater archaeology department was part of Naval History and Heritage Command.

Well, that changed everything. He'd lay odds everyone at NHHC with a connection to the MacLeod-Hill project had been invited to the party. This could be the perfect opportunity for Keith to apologize to the historian.

CHAPTER TWO

TRINA FROWNED AT her reflection. Her day dress was perfect for the party in that it was conservative. Staid. Dull.

Keith Hatcher's jab at her age and appearance still rankled four hours later. She would *not* show up at Dr. Hill's party looking like a twenty-year-old librarian. She threw open her closet and searched through her dresses. Her hand stopped on a red, knee-length cocktail dress she'd never mustered the courage to wear. It showed cleavage, which she only had if she wore the really tight bra she'd bought just for this dress. Plus she'd have to wear a thong to avoid panty lines.

Screw it. She'd wear the miserable bra and underwear and look like an adult for a change. Dr. Hill's assistant would be there, and Trina had harbored a crush on the guy since they started exchanging e-mails for a joint NHHC-MacLeod-Hill PR project. Perry Carlson was good-looking, successful, smart, and had the most important attribute of any potential date: he wasn't in the military.

Because she was a military historian working on a military base, the *only* single men Trina met were in the military, and she'd dated a few of them. She was done with soldiers, sailors, airmen, and marines. Hell, she was done with coast guardsmen too.

Senior Chief Petty Officer Keith Hatcher was a prime example why. Hot as hell and full of himself, he'd belittled her and assumed she was a fool.

No more. Perry Carlson was her ideal guy. Educated, charming. Plus, he respected her. He knew her work was important and could save the lives of servicemen and women in the future. And she'd be lying if she didn't admit Perry's looks were a bonus. He was gorgeous. Not rugged like disheveled Keith, but crisp, handsome.

The last time they'd met, at an event at the Institute, they'd chatted for thirty minutes over glasses of champagne, and she'd been certain he was about to ask her out, when Dr. Hill made some boring announcement that ruined the moment. Perry'd had to run off to assist his boss and failed to follow up on his promise to return and finish their conversation.

But it was a work event for both of them; she understood why she'd been left hanging. And sure, Perry *could* have called her at work and asked her out, but maybe she hadn't given off enough *I'm interested* vibes and he'd been afraid she'd turn him down. A legitimate concern, since it would have made working together on the PR project awkward.

Today would be different. If he didn't ask her out, she'd go for it and ask him. Perry was exactly what she wanted in a man, and she would wear a dress that would show him she was a woman.

She slipped on the painful red bra and cinched it tight. Her meager breasts pulled together as promised. The dress fell into place, snug on the hips and bust. She turned to the mirror, making sure the fabric was smooth. Her body was skinny—a problem many women would love to have, she knew, but her slight frame contributed to everyone thinking she was ten years younger—or more—than she was. She'd never "filled out" during puberty and fit the same cup size she'd worn at fourteen. Eighty-five percent of the time she was content with her body. The other fifteen percent was usually triggered when her shape—or lack thereof—caused men to think she was in her teens.

It was embarrassing to be not just carded when ordering a drink, but questioned—address, astrological sign, and even birthstone—when out on a date, because the server assumed she had a fake ID. It invariably made her date uncomfortable too. She could tell by the way they shifted in their seat that they realized the waiter thought they were out with jailbait.

She twirled in front of the mirror. At least she had a decent butt. With just enough curve to look good in a tight dress, it didn't disappear like her hips.

Dress decision made, what to do about her hair? Thick but dull brown, there wasn't much she could do with it. She was tired of the French twist and decided to try a loose braid, which would keep it off her neck in the summer heat but didn't look too *librarian.*

The one thing she couldn't change was her glasses. She'd tried contact lenses several times over the years, but they hurt like hell.

She'd given up and accepted her fate, choosing cute glasses in fun colors. So the glasses remained, but she chose the red-rimmed ones that matched her dress, then made a face at her reflection. She'd been feeling insecure about her appearance ever since meeting Keith Hatcher this morning, and the berating internal monologue needed to stop.

I am a smart, powerful adult woman. If I don't respect myself, no one else will.

She stuck her tongue out at her reflection, an action that was neither powerful nor adult, but it did make her smile.

Keith Hatcher's opinion of her looks didn't define her. She knew who she was, inside and out, and no man's two-second assessment should override her sense of self-worth. Yet the half-naked man she'd barely spoken to had gotten into her head.

Ridiculous. He was a source for information and nothing more. Unfortunately, she *would* face him again. Hatcher was her ticket away from spending her days analyzing World War II US Naval ship movements. Her account of the Navy's action in Somalia would be beneficial to future troops and ensure the mistakes made there would never be repeated.

At least, she assumed there had been mistakes in Somalia. Why else would they give her the assignment? It also explained Hatcher's reluctance to talk.

She'd already immersed herself in the details: the attitude of the Somali government toward al Qaeda, the rival warlords and interclan violence that gave rise to the terrorist leader and the villagers who'd protected him. There had also been a UN peacekeepers camp, charged with protecting refugees who'd fled a warlord who had clashed with the al Qaeda leader. It should have been a case of *the enemy of my enemy is my friend*, but nothing was that simple in Somalia or with al Qaeda. As far as she could tell, the warlords had no concept of friend or ally.

She'd thought her new level of security clearance made the assignment a slam dunk, but she hadn't counted on facing down a recalcitrant SEAL. Actually, several recalcitrant SEALs—no one on his team would talk to her. She'd hoped that because she hadn't received an outright "no" to her e-mails, Keith Hatcher would be the exception.

Ready for the party, she knocked on her guest bedroom door. She'd rented out the extra room to an NHHC summer intern,

Cressida Porter, who she liked a lot, but Trina was disappointed Cressida's boyfriend was visiting for the weekend just so he could attend the party. Not because she didn't like Todd, but because having set her sights on Perry, Trina needed a wingwoman, and with her boyfriend in tow, Cressida wasn't available for the job.

"Cress? You and Todd ready?"

The bedroom door opened. Cressida looked gorgeous in an orange day dress that looked fabulous against her olive complexion. Her brown eyes and broad smile always reminded Trina of the actress Natalie Portman. Cressida looked pretty even rumpled and groggy first thing in the morning, which just wasn't fair.

"Wow, your dress is hot," Cressida said, slipping a small purse over her shoulder. "Do I look okay? God, I'm so nervous."

"You look great. Dr. Hill's parties are easy—there will be enough of us from NHHC there to make it a friendly crowd."

Todd draped an arm around Cressida's shoulder. "I'm living the dream, showing up at the party with two gorgeous women."

It was nice of Todd to include her in the statement, but she would never compare to Cressida's movie-star looks. Not that she wanted to, but sometimes she wished she had the kind of curves a man like Keith Hatcher would notice. Men like that never noticed the skinny, nerdy-historian types.

I do not want a Keith Hatcher type. I want a Perry Carlson type. The Perry Carlsons of the world noticed and appreciated brainy historians.

Her apartment was a third-floor walk-up on the border between the Adams Morgan and Dupont Circle neighborhoods. Because the party was in Annapolis, and neither Cressida nor Trina had a car, her coworker Erica Kesling and her fiancé, Lee Scott, were giving them a ride. As her trio stepped out into the humid summer afternoon, Lee pulled up in front of the building.

She'd met and become fast friends with Erica when Trina was hired at NHHC nearly two years ago. Erica worked in the underwater archaeology division, housed in Building One at the Washington Navy Yard, whereas Trina, Cressida, and Mara worked with the historians and terrestrial archaeologists in the larger adjacent office building.

Cressida and Erica were chatty on the drive to Dr. Hill's estate. The younger intern only had two weeks left in DC before she

would head back to the underwater archaeology graduate program
at Florida State University. Trina would miss her. She'd been a fun
summer roommate and coworker.

"I'm going to try to convince Hill to give us a tour of his two-
person research submarine," Erica said, garnering a squeal of
delight from Cressida. "The Navy is very interested in the
mapping he's been doing off the Carolina coast. There is a
submerged Curtiss SBC Helldiver in the area, and I want to know
if he can get me a pretty image of it with that new side-scan sonar
he's been bragging about."

Todd, also a graduate student in Cressida's program, launched
into praise for the latest developments in side-scan sonar, and the
three underwater archaeologists were off, chattering about things
Trina knew nothing about.

"What's new in history?" Lee asked.

She smiled. Lee was a military history buff and loved hearing
about her research into World War II naval operations. "I'd tell
you, but my current assignment is top secret. So, you know... I'd
have to kill you."

"Finally getting to use that new security clearance? Cool."

The vetting process had taken months, and everyone knew the
clearance was the necessary step if she wanted to finally move up
in the ranks. She had Mara to thank for pushing her application
through. She could have languished as junior historian for a
decade if not for Mara's support.

They arrived at the party, and Erica, Cressida, and Todd went
off in search of Dr. Hill and his magic submarine, leaving Trina to
either stay back with Lee or venture off to find Perry. She decided
to get a drink and play it cool.

Lee glanced toward the outside patio and made a face. "I'm
not in the mood for this today. Wanna play pool?" He nodded
toward the game room to the right, which was just off the large
patio.

She crossed her arms. She'd played pool with Lee before.
"Only if you promise to shoot left-handed."

He grinned. "Deal."

He was probably just as good with his left. They headed into
the empty game room. "I'll get us beers if you rack," he offered.

She nodded and grabbed the triangle. She'd relax, shoot some
pool, drink some beer, and then head out in search of Perry.

Maybe, if she were lucky, Perry would wander in and join the game. Yes. That would be better. Fun. Casual.

She was determined to make her move today.

Ψ

KEITH FROWNED AS he circled the patio. No sign of his sexy historian anywhere. The Navy contingent at the party was high—but then, with the proximity to the Academy, he'd expected that.

He finally caught sight of Rav, three-deep behind suck-ups who were hedging their bets that the man would be the next junior senator from Maryland. He caught Rav's eye, and his friend grinned, extracted himself from the sycophants, and greeted him with a pat on the back. "I didn't think you'd show."

"Well, there's a woman I'm hoping is here."

Rav rolled his eyes. "Figures. Do I know her?"

"No clue. She works for Mara Garrett at NHHC. She's an historian."

"Good. For a second, I thought you were going to say she's an archaeologist, and I was going to warn you to stay the hell away."

"That's right, the nut job who's giving you trouble with the Alaska compound is an archaeologist. Is the compound still closed?"

"That's what I wanted to talk to you about—and why I want you to meet Curt." Rav nodded toward the house. "He's inside, getting his ass kicked at pool. C'mon. I'll introduce you. Mara's in there, so maybe your historian is there too."

Keith followed Rav through a sliding glass door into a large room with a pool table in the center. Along the side of the room were vintage pinball machines and a sweet old Wurlitzer jukebox.

After a quick scan of the occupants of the room, he forgot all about Hill's expensive toys. He recognized the gorgeous ass in the tight red dress bent over the rail and smiled. She took a shot, and her cue was true. A striped ball rolled into the pocket, and Trina straightened and high-fived the tall man by her side.

Holy shit, if he'd thought her sexy in the buttoned-up blouse and prim skirt, she was smoking now in a snug dress that highlighted her slim figure and revealed a little cleavage. He found himself stupid jealous of the tall man who was now giving her tips on how to line up her next shot.

"That's enough coaching, Lee," said a man who stood on the

opposite side of the table with a cue in hand. "Trina's kicking my ass enough as it is." Keith recognized him as Curt Dominick. The man caught sight of Rav and said, "Alec, you done sucking up yet? I could use your help here."

Rav made a face. "I wish."

Trina and the tall man turned to face the door. Trina's eyes widened, and she let slip a faint gasp.

Keith liked being the cause of that slight intake of breath. For the second time today, he watched her cheeks redden, but this time, she couldn't bolt down the stairs and get away. No, she had to face him, and he liked her flustered reaction. He liked even more that she didn't lean toward the man by her side. If the guy were her boyfriend, she sure as hell would make it clear in front of Keith. But the man and Dominick were both focused on Rav. No one but Keith seemed to notice Trina's distress.

She stepped back and murmured something to another woman—Mara Garrett?—then handed over her stick and left the room without a word. Keith's gaze followed her until she slipped out of sight in the garden.

"Trina's your historian?" Rav asked.

He nodded.

Rav snickered. "Clearly not yours, though, given her quick exit."

"Give me time, man. The party is young."

Mara Garrett studied him from across the room, her gaze speculative.

Keith faced the men he was ostensibly here to talk to and was introduced to Lee Scott and Curt Dominick. "So, what's going on with the Alaska compound?" Keith asked, referring to a state-of-the-art military training ground that Rav had acquired when he purchased Raptor, a private security and tactical training organization.

"It's going to reopen the first week of September," Rav said. "Lee is flying out next week to go over the computer security. Someone hacked the system, but I don't think it's the woman who's been lobbying to get the training ground shut down permanently."

"Why not?"

"As far as I can tell," Lee said, "she doesn't have the necessary skills. It's a sophisticated hack, and while the woman is clearly smart, she's no techie."

Keith nodded. "And what do you want from me?"

Rav smiled. "I want you to consider giving up your premature and lazy-assed retirement. I need you at Raptor." He nodded toward Dominick. "And for the position I'm thinking of, Curt here needs to vet you."

The attorney general was doing background checks? This was no petty security guard position Rav was offering. Keith knew Dominick had vetted Rav personally—that was how the two men had met—before the government approved Rav's purchase of the company after it had been seized from the previous owners. The attorney general, his wife, and Raptor had bad history.

"I don't know, Rav. I'm liking my lazy-assed premature retirement."

"Bullshit. You're antsy as hell and just hoping to drive up the offer—before I've even made it."

"Will it work?"

"It might." Rav sighed. "I've got to go outside and resume the glad-handing. Can we talk tomorrow? Noon. My office?"

"Sure."

Rav nodded and left.

Keith hung back and chatted with the others, wondering how long he had to stay before he could pursue Trina without looking pathetic.

Mara fixed him with an assessing look. "How do you know Trina?"

The woman's boss didn't know Trina had asked him about Somalia? That was…interesting. "Through the Navy," he said, which was both cryptic and true. Since his interest in Trina must have been obvious, he decided looking pathetic was better than feeling antsy, and he set off to find her.

ψ

TRINA'S HEART POUNDED, and not because she was approaching Perry. Keith Hatcher was *here*. Her body had gone into a full-blown awkward-schoolgirl reaction. She'd flushed and felt short of breath.

She had a *crush* on Keith Hatcher? That was…insane.

Sure, he was hot. But he was also condescending and rude. There was nothing there to like. But she needed to convince her body of that, because she was ready to hyperventilate. And it wasn't from anger. No. The trigger was pure excited anticipation.

Surely she anticipated talking to Perry again. Yes. It wasn't Hatcher who had made her heart rate pick up. No way.

Perry was deep in conversation with Dr. Hill and another man, so Trina scanned the crowd for someone else to talk to. With the exception of Erica and Todd, who were talking to another MacLeod-Hill Institute bigwig, everyone Trina knew was inside playing pool. She hated standing alone at parties, and her discomfort only intensified at the notion of Keith seeing her out here pitifully alone.

What the hell was Keith Hatcher doing here? And how did he know Alec Ravissant? Months ago, she'd met Alec at a dinner party at Mara's house but didn't know him well.

She headed for the open bar and requested a glass of red wine. Another man stepped up beside her and ordered a drink, then turned to her as they both waited. "I don't think we've met. I'm Derrick Vole. I work for Alec Ravissant."

Tall and skinny with endearing freckles but not a lot of muscle, he didn't look like the typical Raptor operative. "For Raptor?" she asked, then flushed, realizing her disbelief was evident in her voice.

Fortunately, the man chuckled. "No. The senate campaign."

She smiled. "Sorry. Trina Sorensen, Naval History and Heritage Command." She held out her hand, which he took in a firm grip.

"There are several of you here today. I was just talking to your coworker, Walt Fryer."

Trina hid her frown as she accepted her wineglass from the bartender and moved to the side to continue the conversation. *Oh goody. Walt's here.* Walt was an old-school historian who didn't truck with the idea of women being military historians. He'd flipped when Mara was promoted to interim director of the history program less than a year ago, and cried favoritism when Mara pushed for Trina's security clearance.

But hypocrisy hadn't stopped him from dumping his work on her as soon as she'd passed muster. Walt was a piece of work and her least favorite person in the department.

"I'm in charge of arranging events for Rav." Derrick cleared his throat. "Excuse me, Alec—"

Trina smiled at his formality; she knew Alec's nickname.

"—and after talking to Walt, I was thinking of arranging a tour at the history museum at the Navy Yard. Maybe round up some old vets and make it a photo op."

"That should be easy to arrange. The museum is pretty quiet during the week."

Derrick handed her his card. "I'd appreciate your help in setting it up. Maybe next week?"

"I can try to help, but I'm afraid I don't work for the museum. I'm an historian."

He gave her a look that likely mirrored the one she'd given him when he said he worked for Alec and he didn't fit her mold for a Raptor operative. Turnabout was fair play, and in this instance, she was just as guilty of making assumptions based on appearance. "Really? I assumed you were an administrative assistant or an intern at the museum. I mean, you're so young, and Walt said you're the person to talk to for tours."

She rolled her eyes. "That sounds like the Walt I know and love."

Cressida appeared by her side. "It looks like Dr. Hill is going to give a handful of NHHC people rides in his sub—maybe even before I return to Tallahassee. Do you want to put your name in for the tour?" she asked.

Trina suppressed a shudder. "No way. I'd get claustrophobic in a two-person sub." She did not understand how archaeologists could find joy in all things buried or underwater. She'd take an oral interview or written account to tell her the past any day.

Derrick exchanged pleasantries with Cressida, then said he'd call Trina to arrange the tour and moved on. As soon as he was out of earshot, Trina said, "Walt just demoted me to museum docent."

"At least docenting is fun. Wait, can docent be a verb?"

"It will be when I do it. I will verb the hell out of that job."

Cressida laughed. Walt and Erica approached from across the lawn. From the look on Erica's face, she wasn't enjoying Walt's company much either.

"Trina!" he said as if they were long lost friends. "I've been hoping to talk to you. I think one of my sources for a study of the UN coalition post-Desert Storm would respond better to a girl. I'd like you to interview him."

She bit her tongue to keep from pointing out she wasn't a *girl* any more than he was a *boy*. "I'm sort of swamped right now, Walt, what with all the other projects you shifted to me in the last weeks."

He waved a hand. "Those are all small. A quick report for the department, a few paragraphs for the *Pull Together* newsletter, and you're done. Hell, I'm surprised you haven't finished them already."

She narrowed her gaze. Ninety percent of the time, she thought Walt was clueless, but the other ten she was certain he was a calculating bastard who knew exactly what he was doing and saying. "Not all the sources are being cooperative."

"I scheduled the interview for Tuesday morning. I'll e-mail you with the details." He walked away before she could protest.

"I can't wait until he retires," Erica said.

"Be glad you aren't in the cubicle next to his."

"I say a word of thanks every time I visit you." Erica shot a glare toward Walt over her shoulder. "Tell Mara he was heavy-handed and skip the interview. It's his job, not yours."

Trina shrugged, unsure of how she'd handle it. If her schedule was free Tuesday morning, she didn't really have a reason to say no. Her hire at NHHC was conditional. Until she reached the three-year mark, she had to toe a certain line, and Walt knew it. He was a technical GS-14, a higher pay grade and seniority level than everyone in the department, including Mara.

Most likely, Trina would do the interview, and she'd smile as she did it to hide her gritting teeth.

She took another sip of her wine. Over Cressida's shoulder, she noted Perry was with Dr. Hill and Alec Ravissant. As soon as he broke away, she'd make her move.

She caught sight of Keith approaching out of the corner of her eye and felt a tingling sensation at the back of her neck. She wanted to flirt with Perry, but *Keith* was giving her goose bumps? What was *wrong* with her? He reached her side, and she glanced at him askance. "Well, Hatcher. You do clean up pretty."

He laughed.

She turned to him, giving him her full attention. A scan from head to toe had her wishing her words weren't true. He looked *good*. Really good. And she'd had no complaints about his appearance this morning when he was sleep rumpled and half-naked.

Well, she might even prefer him sleep rumpled and half-naked. Just the thought made her body heat.

Dammit.

He wore a simple button-down shirt and tan slacks, his broad shoulders and fine physique readily apparent even when covered. His short, dark hair no longer jutted up on one side; it was brushed back and revealed just a hint of curl. He smelled good too—a musky cologne that made her want to bite him.

He's military. Not your type. He doesn't respect you. He probably thinks you're a twit simply because you are a woman.

She'd met enough men like that to last her.

"Trina, you left my house so fast this morning, I worried I'd never see you again."

Erica looked at her sharply. The man made it sound like she'd snuck out after a one-night stand. Cressida merely looked confused, but then, as her roommate, she knew Trina had woken up in her own bed this morning.

She glared at him and pointed to a private corner of the garden. "Over there. Now."

Hatcher grinned. "I love a woman who takes charge."

Trina let out a frustrated sigh as she led him to the secluded corner. "Please, Senior Chief, those are my coworkers. Don't give them the wrong idea about you and me."

He smiled, giving his eyes a sexy heat. "Please, call me Keith. And I didn't say anything that was inaccurate."

"Keith, why are you here?"

"I read your e-mail after you left this morning. All of them, actually. I didn't receive them because... It's a long story and not relevant. But your e-mails made me realize you weren't just showing up out of the blue on a Sunday morning. And I not only came on strong, I was a total ass. I wanted to say I'm sorry."

His words caught her off guard. Honestly, even though she agreed he'd been an ass, she hadn't really felt she deserved an apology. She *did* barge into his house uninvited on a Sunday morning, after all, and it wasn't as if she wasn't aware that SEALs had to be closemouthed about their ops. "Thank you. This is...unexpected. And nice."

His smile was softer now, subtle, and somehow warmer. "I enjoyed meeting you this morning. You were quick, even when I was being a jerk."

What was he saying? That he was *interested* in her? "Well, I work for the military. I'm used to your type."

"Dollface, I'm not a type. I'm one of a kind."

Ahh. There was the man she'd met this morning. She'd been wondering where he'd gone. She rolled her eyes and fought a smile. "Thanks for the apology, Senior Chief. Now, if you're done, I have people I need to talk to."

"Wait." He caught her arm as she turned. "I didn't come here just to apologize. I'd...like to see you again."

Wow. She'd hadn't taken him for the direct type. Then again, offering to masturbate in front her had been pretty damn direct, but he'd been trying to scare her off, not turn her on.

Admittedly, he'd done both.

"You expect me to believe you came all the way out to Annapolis to what... Ask me out?"

He cocked his head. "I don't expect you to believe it, but it's true."

"You were talking with Alec. You know him. That's why you're here."

"I was invited because I know Alec. I came because I guessed you'd be here. So what do you say, Trina? Want to have dinner with me?" He paused, then added, "Now?"

She cocked an eyebrow. He couldn't be serious. "You mean leave the party?"

"Yes."

She hesitated and couldn't believe she even considered his offer. This was a pseudowork event. And she'd come here intending to flirt with Perry.

Perry. Crap. She hadn't even tried to talk to him yet. Perry, who was her type. Perry, who respected her.

She frowned. "I'd say yes to dinner with Senior Chief Hatcher so we could talk about the Somalia op. I don't think I could handle Keith, who wants to ditch the party."

"You don't have to *handle* me." His smile turned just a bit wicked, telling her exactly where those words sent his thoughts. He shook his head. "It's just dinner. A conversation. Where it goes from there is up to you."

But the very fact he said that left the door open for it to go *somewhere*. "You're very...direct. I didn't expect that."

He held her gaze. "I'm always direct. I have no patience for games or bullshit."

She could be direct too. "Will you tell me about Somalia?"

"No."

"Then I'm sorry, but no thanks." She turned and walked away, shocked she had the nerve to do it. She was ten times a fool, because who knew if he'd change his mind over dinner. But he didn't have patience for games, and she couldn't stomach them. She couldn't go out to dinner with a man because she wanted something from him. But still, she couldn't help but regret having a conscience.

ψ

KEITH WATCHED HER walk away, taking in the swing of her ass that told him what her answer had not—she was interested. She wanted him to notice her.

And he did. Now more than ever.

He had to respect her clarity of purpose. She wasn't going to flirt with him, hoping he'd melt under her feminine wiles. Good call on her part, because no matter how sexy she was, no matter how far things between them went, he'd never, ever talk about Somalia. Not with her. Not with anyone.

Trina approached Dr. Hill, but her eyes were on the man by his side. Polished and slick, the man hung next to the host with an air of pompous importance. Or maybe Keith just felt that way because Trina had made a beeline for him after turning him down cold. And she looked at the guy like he was dinner.

He was probably highly educated, like her. If he hung out with Hill, he must be some sort of scientist. Shit. That guy was her type in a way Keith would never be.

ψ

PERRY CARLSON WAS a pompous bore. How had she never noticed that before?

It might be because the last time they'd chatted, he'd sipped only a single glass of champagne, but today he'd had quite a bit more to drink, and while he appeared composed, his tongue was clearly loosened by alcohol, exposing his braggart tendencies.

Then there was the fact that perhaps she had seen only what she wanted to see. And the person she wanted him to be had nothing to do with the reality of who Perry Carlson was.

But finally, and perhaps most interesting to Trina, was that a man who caused her neck to tingle and was anything but a bore had just told her he was interested, and now she found it hard to muster even the shallow attraction she'd harbored for Perry Carlson.

Shit. She should have taken Keith up on the dinner invitation. She could be with him right now in the dark corner of a romantic restaurant, eating bread dredged in herbs, oil, and vinegar and listening to his SEAL training stories. But no. She was stuck, cornered behind a ridiculous cherub fountain and topiary mermaid.

Seriously, a mermaid?

What was it with underwater explorers and their fascination with breasts and fins? The mermaid's mammary glands were *huge*—not exactly streamlined like, say, a fish's body. And don't get her started on the fact that having breasts meant she'd be a *mammal* with a need to breathe air, like her dolphin and whale counterparts.

And everyone knew mermaids didn't breathe air, ergo mermaids didn't have double-D breasts.

She'd give anything to extract herself from this hidden corner. Unfortunately, Perry wasn't getting the hint. He leaned into her, hints of his quiet inebriation in his bloodshot eyes and whiskey breath. "I'm giving a lecture at the American History Museum next weekend. If you're interested in coming, I could arrange for you to receive a private tour of the collections in storage." He reached out and took the end of her braid and twirled it between his fingers, making her wish she'd chosen to wear it up.

"Thank you, that's very kind, but I interned at the Smithsonian in several different departments when I was in graduate school. I've not only seen the storage, I've cataloged and conserved various items."

"Right. I forgot you studied history."

What the hell? They'd met through her work. As an *historian.* She searched for a response but was more than a little taken aback. Finally, she said, "What's the topic of your lecture?"

"The role of cartographers in World War II." That made sense, given that the mission of Hill's Institute was exploration and mapping—and not just underwater. Perry launched into his subject. "In this day of GPS, many people don't know how important mapmakers were during World War II. You probably don't know some of our most important spies were cartographers."

She must have entered some sort of alternate dimension. What had she ever seen in this guy? "Actually, I did know that."

"Really? Are you interested in military history?"

She took a step back. Was this party being held in Alice's rabbit hole? Drunk or not, his words didn't make sense. "You could say that. I do have a PhD in military history."

"You do?" His eyes—slightly glazed—focused on the cleavage she'd crammed herself into a torturous bra to achieve. She regretted that choice now, because instead of his appreciation triggering a jolt of desire, it left her cold.

She frowned. *Be careful what you wish for.* "Perry, I'm confused. You've been to my office. Where I work for the Navy. As an historian."

"Well, yeah. But... Don't take this the wrong way, but I have it on good authority you were a token hire. NHHC needed a woman historian."

Wow. Okay, he'd earned one point for using the word woman instead of girl (but it was more a sign of how screwed-up the men in her world were that he actually *earned* a point for something that shouldn't even warrant notice). But token hire? Minus ten thousand points. No, a million.

Dammit. His "good authority" had to be Walt. The sexist jerk probably even believed his own fabrication. She'd worked damn hard to earn her spot at NHHC and was probably a better historian than many of her male counterparts—especially myopic old bastards like Walt.

Unfortunately, Perry's attitude was nothing new, but for some stupid reason she hadn't expected it from him. Perhaps he was guilty of the same thing she'd done, seeing what he wanted to see—and he'd wanted to see a woman who was too dim-witted to realize she was a token hire.

That so was not her. On so many levels.

She turned to leave. She was done talking to him.

He grabbed her arm. "Wait, Trina. Are you mad? I didn't mean to cause offense. If I did, I'm sorry."

"You're only sorry *if* you caused offense? Because if my feeble woman's brain can't grasp how sexist you are, then you don't have to feel bad?" She wanted to add *for being a pig* but refrained. She was classy that way.

Perry's grip on her arm was firm. She tried to pull away but couldn't break the hold. "Hey, I'm sorry if you didn't know—"

"Is everything okay, Trina?" Keith asked, stepping up beside her.

Trina closed her eyes, trying to decide if she was mortified or thankful Keith had witnessed Perry's douchebaggery. The last thing she needed was to be rescued, but at the same time, Perry *did* have her arm in his tight fist, and she had no clue how to get him to let go without causing an embarrassing scene. The mermaid's breasts could only hide so much.

Plus, if Perry claimed she was a token one more time, she might just slug him.

"This is between Trina and I," Perry said. "Go away."

"Trina and me," Keith corrected, then he leaned in close and dropped his voice so only Trina and Perry could hear. "And you need to let go of Trina right now, or it will be between you and *me*."

Perry released her and she rubbed her arm. His grip had slowly tightened, and she wondered if she'd have a bruise tomorrow.

Perry glared at Keith. "Who are you?"

"I'm the guy who's taking her home." Keith turned to Trina. "Dollface, you ready to go?"

She'd say yes to almost anything to get away from Perry Carlson, so much that she wasn't even ticked off by the implication she was going from here to Keith's bed. "Sure."

"He calls you dollface, yet *I'm* the sexist one?" Perry asked.

Trina frowned. He had a point, sort of. Both men had been condescending to her at one time or another today. But Keith—he'd apologized. A real apology, taking the onus of his behavior on himself. Whereas Perry's apology had been conditional—he was only sorry if she'd taken offense.

Plus, she had a feeling Keith only called her dollface when he was playing the role of cocky SEAL. That wasn't all there was to Keith. At least she didn't think so.

Hell, what did she know? If someone had asked her this morning which man would bore, insult, and offend her, and which one would apologize, rescue, and intrigue her, she'd have guessed wrong.

She shrugged and took a step toward Keith. Perry caught her by the other arm. "Wait, Trina. After last time... I thought...maybe there was something between us. Admit it, you wore that dress for me. Not this asshole."

She hated that he was right about the dress, but he'd never hear that from her. She tried to jerk her arm from his grasp and failed. "Sorry, Perry. Not interested."

Keith stepped closer to Perry. "Don't do this, man. This isn't the time or place."

"You think I'm afraid of you?"

"I don't give a shit if you're afraid of me. I'm not the one with something to lose here."

Perry released her arm. She rubbed her bicep, certain she'd have matching bruises tomorrow. "Let's go," she said to Keith.

"Uptight, dippy bitch. Hell, you aren't my type anyway. I prefer women with curves."

Keith stopped and closed his eyes as if seeking patience. He opened them and said, "Trina, can I hit him? *Please?*"

"He's drunk. And an ass. Not really worth the trouble it would cause."

Keith nodded and took a step toward the game room.

"Pussy," Perry said.

They'd given the man every opportunity, and he'd squandered each one. Somehow, insulting Keith crested her breaking point. She twisted on her heel and took a swing, only to be stopped by Keith's quick grasp. His hand curled around her wrist and gently pulled her back. "As you said, he's not worth it."

CHAPTER THREE

KEITH WAS STUNNED Trina had taken a swing at the prick. He'd managed to stop her on instinct alone. He shifted his hold on her forearm—far more gently than the guy she'd tried to deck—and led her through the garden to the house and out through the front door.

She shook her head as if just realizing her surroundings. "We can't leave."

"You sure as hell aren't staying."

"My friends—"

"Saw that you're with me when we passed through the house."

She glanced back at the front door. Nothing was going as planned today. "I can't leave with you."

He couldn't let her go back. She was riding adrenaline, and he'd bet good money she wasn't used to it, didn't realize a crash was coming. Plus the last thing she needed was to explain the bullshit she'd put up with from whoever that prick was to her friends, especially since one of those friends was her boss.

She turned to head back into the house.

"If you come with me, you can ask me three questions about Somalia," he blurted. It was the only thing he could think of to stop her.

She paused. "You have a car?"

He nodded and darted down the steps to the valet stand. "Black Toyota Land Cruiser. No top."

The boy took off to get his rig, and moments later, Keith was behind the wheel with Trina in the passenger seat. He maneuvered down the twisting drive and pulled out onto the rural road on the outskirts of Annapolis. The late-afternoon summer sun shone down, he had the top off his Cruiser, and there was a beautiful woman in his passenger seat. He felt more anticipation for...*life*...than he had in months. Certainly since leaving the Navy.

She flopped back in the seat, turning her face toward the sun. Her half smile lit an unfamiliar fire in his belly.

"Have you ever punched someone before?" he asked.

She glanced at him through the corner of her eye. Her mouth curved another fraction of an inch. "Yes."

He did a double take. Trina was full of surprises.

"I was impressed with how you tried to defuse him," she said. "That you didn't rise to his bait. Sorry I blew it."

He shrugged. "Better men than him have baited me. And I held back for you. I figured you didn't want a scene. Not with your boss there."

She lost the content smile and sat up straighter. "Yeah. I didn't."

"Odds are, no one saw you take the swing. There was a gigantic mermaid in the way. And the guy sure as hell won't mention it."

"I'm screwed if Dr. Hill saw us. He consults with the Navy a lot, and Erica was trying to convince him to share some important mapping data. Perry is his golden-boy assistant. I may have to lay low in the history department for a while."

"So what's the deal? Were you into that guy?"

"I thought I was, until he drank too much. Good lord, he was so full of himself. I've written dozens of articles and a book on military history. Which I know he has a copy of because I gave it to him when he visited my office. Yet he thinks *I'm* a token. I may not be Doris Kearns Goodwin, but I'm no slouch in my field. As if the Navy would pay me to sit in my cubicle and do nothing just because I have ovaries."

Keith took his eyes off the road. Warm color lit her cheeks. Moral outrage looked good on her.

Everything looked good on her.

"Crap!" She bolted upright. "We have to go back."

"Why?"

"I left my purse in Erica's car. My ID, phone, keys, money. I don't have anything."

He pulled his cell out of his pocket and handed it to her. "Call Erica. Ask her if you can pick it up later tonight from her place."

"What do I do until then?"

"I'm taking you out to dinner."

"I suppose she could give it to Cressida—my roommate. After

Cressida gets home, I could get into the apartment."

"Perfect."

Trina made the call and was grateful to leave a message on Erica's cell. The last thing she wanted was to answer questions right then. She set the phone on the console and said, "We have one problem. I don't have ID. I *always* get carded, and frankly, I would really like a stiff drink right now."

Keith grinned. "Well then, you've just given me the perfect excuse to take you back to my place." An image of her splayed out in his bed flashed in his mind. His fingers tightened on the steering wheel. "If that's okay with you."

She looked at him speculatively. "Can you cook?"

"Babe, I'm the youngest of four boys. It was learn to cook, or starve."

"Good, because I can't. Your place it is."

He pulled a U-turn in the middle of the empty country road. The sun was shining, the top was off, he had a job offer on the table from Rav, and a beautiful woman had just agreed to go back to his place. Not a bad result from a party he hadn't even wanted to attend.

TRINA COULDN'T BELIEVE she was back in Keith's town house only nine hours after she'd fled this morning. It was a dangerous place to be, considering she'd come down from a slight adrenaline rush, and all she wanted to do was drag the man up to his bedroom and take advantage of him.

It didn't help that his living room contained her ultimate aphrodisiac—one entire wall was loaded floor-to-ceiling bookshelves. She studied the feast, running her hands along the spines, realizing with a jolt that the nonfiction books were organized according to Dewey. She shifted to the fiction section and noted those books were organized by genre and author.

What kind of man did that?

The same man with a mudroom that lacked mud and a kitchen without crumbs.

She plucked a paperback copy of one of her favorite Truman biographies from the shelf and admired the gently worn spine. Either he'd bought it used or he'd read it.

She opened to the title page and felt a strange flutter to see the author had signed the book with an inscription to Keith. The soft thud of footsteps on the carpet told her he had entered the room. She turned to face him. Damn if he didn't look even more appealing now that she knew he not only read biographies, he went to signings to meet the authors. Was there *anything* sexier than that?

He handed her a glass of red wine. "That's a great book, but have you read this one?" He set down his own wineglass and plucked a history of the battle of Peleliu from the shelves.

She nodded. "It's heartbreaking. Sledge's account is the definitive story, but I appreciate that one for the historical perspective, which you can't get from a first-person account." She slid the biography back into its slot and sipped the wine. Heat infused her, and she felt a slight buzz that couldn't have anything to do with wine she'd only just sipped, but had everything to do with Keith.

"Sledge puts you in the battle, no doubt about that, but sometimes I find the first-person account too narrow."

She waved her hand to indicate his library. "You read a lot of history."

"I went from high school straight to the Navy." He cleared his throat as if embarrassed. "Reading makes up for my lack of education."

"You served in the Navy for nearly thirteen years and completed multiple deployments to Iraq and Afghanistan. Your life experience is worth ten times my PhD."

He glanced down, making her wonder if he felt self-conscious and if she'd just said the worst thing possible. He could think she was being condescending, but she'd meant it. She had absolute respect for every man and woman who donned a uniform and served.

"Is pasta with mushroom sauce okay?" he asked in an obvious change of subject. "Everything else is frozen."

"Sounds perfect." If she was botching this with words, she'd stop talking. She set her wineglass on the shelf next to his and took a step closer.

He flashed a sexy smile. "Careful, Trina. I might forget about dinner."

She felt a little reckless and leaned into him, breathed in his scent. He wore some awesome aftershave that practically caused a nose orgasm. She placed her hands flat on his pecs and slid upward, loving the feel of his firm body through his shirt. She surprised herself with her forwardness. She was usually the type to wait for the guy to make a move. But she felt strangely impatient, and from Keith's heated gaze, she knew he'd didn't mind being on the receiving end of her advances.

He dropped the book on the floor and slid both hands around her waist, pulling her snug against him. "Screw it. I'll order a pizza."

She laughed and rose up on her toes. He leaned down to meet her halfway, and his lips found hers. Heat unfurled with the first invasion of his tongue. Her mouth moved under his, his tongue slid along hers, and she wanted to purr with the warm, wonderful sensation. She stroked his cheek, so sexy smooth; he must have shaved right before the party.

She opened her mouth wider, and he delved deeper. It was a good thing his arms circled her waist, because her legs turned to jelly, or maybe she just forgot how to stand. He caught her as she started to drop and plucked her up, carrying her to the sofa without breaking the kiss.

He sat so she straddled him. Her short dress rode up, allowing her center to press directly against his erection with only her insignificant thong and his slacks between them. The pressure felt insanely good. She lifted her head and wiggled her hips, increasing the friction. "I'm really glad you came to the party, Senior Chief."

He dropped nipping kisses along her collarbone, then his lips trailed lower, into the V of her cleavage. "Me too," he said against her skin.

"And leaving was a good idea too. This is way better than making small talk with stuffy politicos."

He unzipped the back of her dress. "This is way better than just about anything. Ever."

She chuckled and found the top button of his shirt. "So you don't think I'm fooling around with you just to get information, I suppose I should ask my three questions now."

She felt his body tense between her thighs. Dammit. She'd said that wrong. She stroked his cheek and said, "I like you, Keith. That's why I kissed you. It has nothing to do with my research into Somalia. I wouldn't do that."

His gaze didn't leave hers. "I know."

She leaned down and kissed him again, but his lips were stiff. He kissed her back, but without the heat of a moment before. She slid from his lap and stood. "Let's just get the questions over with, then." She dropped back onto the sofa, leaving two feet between them. "Was your team able to infiltrate the al Qaeda leader's stronghold?"

Keith closed his eyes and rubbed a hand across his face. "I can't answer that."

"You promised. And I have the necessary clearance. You can tell me everything."

"I didn't promise anything. I only said you could *ask* three questions. I never said I'd answer them."

His words snapped the hazy spell that had enveloped her from the moment she took in his bookshelves. She jumped to her feet. "You sonofabitch!"

"Trina. I *can't* talk about my ops. I swore an oath."

She clenched her jaw. "I. Have. Clearance. You can tell me."

"I've been debriefed. I don't have to tell you anything."

How could she be so stupid? She'd been eager to escape the mess she'd made of the party, and had glommed on to his promise. She felt like a fool.

"Trina, I like you. I want to spend time with you. Date you. Make love to you. But you need to understand, I will never tell you about any of the ops I was involved in with the SEALs. Period."

"I'm such an idiot." She was stuck in Falls Church without so much as a Metro farecard to get her home. "I need five dollars."

"What?"

"Five dollars. So I can take the Metro home."

"I thought this"—he indicated his open shirt, her gaping dress—"had nothing to do with your research into Somalia. There's no reason for you to leave."

She zipped the back of her dress. "And I thought you didn't play games. I lost my libido when I realized you misled me. I no longer find you attractive."

"Bullshit."

"You've got an impressive ego, Senior Chief. You may be hot, but no amount of muscle can make up for being manipulative. Now, I need five dollars or a farecard."

"I'll give you a ride. After dinner. If we leave now, your

roommate won't be home yet. You're locked out."

"I don't give a damn. Give me five dollars, or I'll walk."

"Trina—"

"You're no better than Perry. In fact, you're worse. He was a sexist pig and condescending, but at least he was upfront about it." She grabbed Keith's landline and started to dial.

"Who are you calling?"

She twisted, turning her back to him. "Cressida. I'm letting her know I'm on my way home."

"It's getting dark. Where do you live? You can't walk home from a Metro station alone. At least let me take you home." His voice was low, his tone regretful.

She gripped the phone tighter, afraid he'd try to take it from her. "Do you really think I'd get in a car with you again? Not just no, but hell, no."

He didn't say a word as she spoke to Cressida, and in the end, he gave her the five dollars. She hadn't counted on him following her out the door and down the street. Or riding the Metro with her. He sat at the opposite end of the train car and exited when she exited, switching to the Red Line when she switched. He followed her down the busy streets near DuPont Circle, maintaining a discreet distance, and waited a block away as she sat on her front stoop and waited for Cressida.

His presence was strangely comforting; she hated walking the last two blocks to her place alone at night. Forty-five minutes passed as darkness deepened, and still, Keith didn't take a step closer, nor did he take a step away. Finally, Cressida and Todd arrived and jumped out of Lee's SUV. Trina waved as he and Erica drove off, then she stood and climbed the stairs to her apartment. She could only assume Keith turned and headed back to the Metro. She didn't bother to look his way as she entered her apartment building.

CHAPTER FOUR

MONDAYS WERE RARELY fun, but Trina had special reasons to dread this particular one. She'd tried to deck Perry Carlson, who was *only* the senior aide to a man who was as revered as James Smithson, the benefactor whose money created the Smithsonian Institution. Then she'd left the party with a man who was a potential source for an oral history *and* was friends with a potential future senator and for all she knew was buddies with her boss's husband, who just so happened to be the US Attorney General.

Life in DC wasn't for the faint of heart. Or poorly connected.

She was on the receiving end of more than a few curious stares as she entered the office, but she ignored them all. She'd told Cressida the details last night but didn't plan to tell anyone else anything.

Of course, the day didn't get any easier when the bouquet of roses arrived.

They worked on a closed military base, which had been the location of a terrifying mass-shooting event. Security was tight on a slow day, and flower delivery was low priority but required high security. She was called to the walk-in gate, where she had to show ID and explain a gift she hadn't known was coming.

The flowers, two dozen red roses, had been searched. Stems were broken. Buds crushed.

It wasn't pretty.

But still, they smelled nice.

The card said simply: *I'm sorry. —Keith*

A second bouquet triggered the same rigmarole. But security was twice as freaked out, because the basket was a massive floral arrangement. From a different guy. Who was also apologizing. She had no idea what the bright summer flowers would have looked like before they searched the hard foam sponge that was supposed to hold the arrangement together, but they fared even worse than the roses.

And security snickered when they asked why Perry Carlson was also apologizing to her. Only one of the marines even pretended the curiosity was part of the job.

Fed up with the questions and leers, Trina snapped. "He's apologizing because I took a swing at him at a party. And he had it coming."

The marines laughed as if her claim was the most absurd thing they'd ever heard, and she took her flowers and returned to her office.

Then security called to tell her flowers from Derrick Vole had arrived. On the card, he apologized for not realizing she was Dr. Trina Sorensen, and he hoped she'd still be willing to help him arrange a photo op for his boss. He included his phone number and begged her to call him.

That was when Trina's headache began.

"I'm having the crappiest day," she said as she flopped into a seat at a table with Mara, Cressida, and Erica in the cafeteria at noon. "Please, someone, show me a kitten video."

"I don't have kittens, but the beast file cabinet will be moved out of your cubicle this afternoon," Cressida said. "Mara got approval to let me catalogue it."

Trina smiled faintly. This *was* good news. The armored file cabinet took up far too much space, and she'd been saddled with it since she'd started working for the Navy two years ago. The cabinet had been moved from cubicle to cubicle since as long as anyone at NHHC could remember—and some of the historians had been here since the Carter administration—always housed with the newest historian in the group. As far as anyone knew, it had been classified as top secret sometime after World War II and promptly forgotten. It was anyone's guess when the keys were lost or what was in it.

Mara had declared one of her goals while interim director would be to see the file cabinet opened and the contents catalogued, and it was on the list of tasks for Cressida to complete during her internship. But good old Walt Fryer had taken issue, insisting Cressida didn't have the proper clearance. Mara had to appeal to the top brass, who concurred with her opinion that the "intelligence" the file cabinet contained was likely to be blueprints of German U-boats or something else laughably out-of-date.

"Maintenance is going to drill out the locks today," Mara said.

"We should start an office pool over what's inside," Erica said. "I'm hoping for papers from Area 51."

Mara scoffed. "No way. The air force would never let the Navy have anything that useful." She fixed Trina with a knowing smile. "So, Trina, much as I love the flowers you gave me, I think you should know I'm married."

Erica snorted. "Yeah, so what is the deal with the SEAL?"

Trina rubbed her temples. "You didn't just say that."

Erica shrugged. "Unintentional rhyme. But I still want details."

"There's no deal. No details."

"For what it's worth, Alec says great things about Keith," Mara ventured. "He really respects the guy."

"Alec can go to hell. His friend's an ass."

Erica sat back in her chair and studied Trina. "I'm thinking Treen didn't get laid last night. What do you think, Mara?"

"If she did, it was awful," Mara replied. "So which is it? Did you drink too much to enjoy the show, or did he have trouble?" She grinned. "That *could* explain the roses."

Trina nearly spewed her drink. She sort of felt like she should defend Keith's manhood, but decided against it. "He pissed me off before things could get really interesting, and I left."

"Shit. No wonder you're so pissy today," Erica said. "Sweetie, next time, use him for sex, then leave. Because you are no fun today."

She winked at Trina, who couldn't help it and laughed. Then Trina grimaced. "There won't be a next time." She stirred her bowl of stew and wondered why she'd ordered such a heavy meal when she wasn't hungry. "He lied to me."

Her friends all bristled in outraged solidarity, making her feel a tad guilty because she supposed he hadn't lied so much as he'd played her.

But that still pissed her off. She should have known. She should have questioned him immediately. But she'd glommed on to the excuse he gave her to leave the party and ended up feeling like a fool.

"Well, Senior Chief Hatcher is a vast improvement over Perry Carlson," Erica said, filling the silent void. "Please tell me you are done with that infatuation."

Trina felt her cheeks flush. She hated being obvious. "Perry Carlson is a vapid pig. He believes *I* was a token hire. Because, you know, they just give away PhDs in military history to women. As if I didn't have to work twice as hard to get into the program, let alone finish it. And the Navy, they are so known for their eagerness to hire a woman to work in one of their many, many penis-only departments."

"You need a night out," Mara said. "Dancing, or just drinking?"

"Drinking," Trina answered. "Lots and lots of drinking." She glared at the three women: one married, one engaged, the last with a boyfriend who was crazy about her. "And no men."

CHAPTER FIVE

KEITH SAT IN his Cruiser in a parking lot outside Trina's office building and tapped the steering wheel as he debated his next step. He needed to do something big. A grand gesture that would win him another shot with her. He had a feeling the roses hadn't cut it.

Since he couldn't give her the one thing she wanted, what could he do?

The thing he wasn't ready to do was give up and let her go, although that should top his list of options. Something about her had gotten under his skin. Maybe it was the way she stood her ground or the way she called him on his bullshit. All he knew was that if he gave up now, he might be stuck with a lifetime of wondering *what if.* He already had one regret to haunt him. He didn't need to add another one.

His meeting with Rav had been long, informative, and opened a door Keith had never thought would be open to him. If Rav were elected to the Senate, he'd have to hand off the running of Raptor—stepping out completely to avoid Senate ethics violations, because Raptor held government contracts. He'd been searching internally for a replacement, but problems with the Alaska compound meant the best candidate for taking over was needed there for the foreseeable future.

Rav had decided to recruit elsewhere, and he wanted Keith to take over as CEO.

The thought was…mind-blowing.

He was no dummy, but he'd attended all of one week of college. Hell, a big part of him felt Trina, with her PhD, was way out of his league. He knew the Navy. He knew strategy, combat, his M110 rifle, his Sig Sauer P226, and he knew what he'd read over the years to make up for his lack of schooling. He could handle the military training aspect of Raptor, no problem, but budgets, financial reports, all the crap that came with being a CEO?

He'd be in over his head. Big-time.

The job was a natural fit for Rav. He grew up with money and had an undergrad degree from freaking Harvard. Harvard Law had accepted Rav, but he'd shocked his family by choosing the Army instead.

Rav had shown Keith balance sheets, real numbers. It was astonishing how much money Raptor was worth—or rather, would be worth, when the Alaska compound resumed operation—and he was ready to hand over the company to Keith.

Keith wasn't like Rav. His only economics class had been in high school, and while he'd survived calculus, he'd only taken the class so he could spend time with the cute, shy girl who'd tutored after school in the cafeteria.

He'd *always* had a thing for brainy chicks.

But back in his office, Rav had shot down his objections. *"You'll have a staff of people who do understand the financials to break it down for you. You'll be up to speed in no time."*

Then Rav had leaned forward, elbows on his knees, and said, *"Here's the deal, Keith—and the reason I want you more than some MBA from an Ivy League school—I don't care if Raptor makes money, I just need it to not lose money. My goal for the business is to give military personnel extensive combat training that could save their lives. After some soul-searching, I've decided to close the nonlethal weapons development lab. Given the former CEO's proclivities, I couldn't trust the developers or the field test results. I decided to keep the private security division open, because it keeps my operatives fit mentally and physically, and their experiences in that sector can be applied at the training ground. I will never take Raptor public, because then I'm beholden to shareholders and profit, and I couldn't make these types of decisions.*

"But here's my problem, if I'm elected, I can't play any role in the company at all. I need to have blind trust that the person running the company will share my philosophy, and hope for the best. Blind trust isn't easy for me, but I know you. And I know you can relate to what I'm trying to do here. And I know I can trust you. Think about my offer. No need to answer today or this week, but I'd like Curt to get started on the vetting process, if you'll consent to that scrutiny."

Keith had agreed to the intensive background check—well aware that this would be the equivalent of a CIA screening and wouldn't be surprised to find a proctologist on his doorstep when he got home—and promised to think about the job. Now he sat outside Trina's office, feeling a little elated, and, if he were being honest, a lot scared. Rav's offer was more than he'd ever dreamed. An opportunity he'd never expected.

That this career path would make his dad pop a vessel was jelly inside a powdered-sugar donut.

Deep down, he wanted to share his excitement—and even his fear—with someone, and the insane notion of that person being Trina wouldn't let him go.

He'd been on dates since leaving Norfolk and moving to DC when he'd left the Navy, but no one had triggered more than passing interest until Trina. But then, none of the others had brazenly invaded his home and didn't flinch in the face of his overbearing, dickish manner. And what kind of woman kept her cool when a guy made a rude comment about her body, but then took a swing because the guy had called Keith a pussy?

And shit, while he was at it, what about that kiss? Christ. Sweet, hot. She'd filled his arms perfectly and had felt like heaven as she straddled him. Her tight dress had ridden up and revealed she wore a thong underneath, and he'd been in the process of sliding his hands down her back to cup that sexy ass when she'd remembered their deal and halted forward progress.

He'd barely been able to sleep last night after the way she'd ground against him, and damn but now he was sporting wood. No way could he face her in this state. He ran through the unsexiest things he could think of, forcing all thoughts of Trina from his mind.

Decent again, he climbed from his rig. He entered her building and made his way toward her cubicle. He found her hunched over a stack of papers, a pen stuck in her bun and a red pen in her hand. She looked freaking adorable, full-on sexy librarian with her slanted glasses high on her nose, a demure pale top, and dark slacks.

Intent on her work, she hadn't noticed him, and he took the moment to examine her workspace. Books, papers, and notebooks were stacked three feet high from the floor. Her desk was littered with papers, pens, sticky notepads, books, and assorted debris.

This was his first glimpse into Trina's world, and he grinned to realize the woman was a slob. Huh. He'd never really given it much thought but supposed he'd always assumed brainy-librarian types were neat freaks.

He didn't see the roses, but there really wasn't a place for her to put them. He cleared his throat softly in the quiet room, and she glanced up.

Her eyes widened, then narrowed with anger. No telltale flash of heat or other hopeful sign. Just anger. Damn. He'd harbored a faint hope this would be easy. No such luck.

She dropped her pen into an open book and snapped it closed. "What are you doing here?"

"That'll crack the spine," he couldn't help but say. Yeah, so maybe he was a bit OCD. He shook his head. "I'm here to see you."

"How did you get on base?"

He shrugged. "I've served in the Navy my entire adult life. I have ID."

She stood. "Follow me." She led him down the narrow aisle between cubicles. At the end of the corridor, she turned. She glanced through a window into one room, then shook her head and kept walking. Keith saw the room was occupied as he passed the window.

Trina paused in front of an open office door, then leaned in. "Mara? Can I use your office for a second? The conference room is busy." She glared over her shoulder at Keith, then stepped into the room, pulling him inside so Mara could see him.

Mara startled, and Keith was fairly certain she suppressed a smile. "Sure," she said and left the room, closing the door behind her.

The moment they were alone, Trina whirled to face him. "What the hell do you think you're doing? I *work* here. Unless you're here to talk about something related to my work, you are not welcome."

"I considered going to your apartment, but I followed you home last night to make sure you were safe, not to find out where you live, and figured if I used the information in that way, you might think I'm creepy." He frowned, seeing two dozen rather beat-up red roses on a credenza. "Are those the roses I sent?"

She nodded.

"What happened to them?"

"Security searched them."

He couldn't help it and shook his head and laughed. "Shit. I can't even send you a decent apology."

"The roses came out better than the flower arrangement from Perry."

Keith stiffened. "He sent you flowers?" His hand curled into a fist. What if she forgave that bastard?

"They're in Erica's office. Cressida has flowers from one of Alec's employees in the conservation lab."

He frowned. Another guy? He'd have to talk to Alec about that to see if it was something worth worrying about. He took a step toward her. "I'm sorry, Trina. I fucked up. I shouldn't have told you that you could ask about Somalia. I was deceptive, and I knew it. I didn't want you to go back to the party—and not for my sake, but for yours. Honestly, I figured staying would be awkward for you." He sighed. "Is there anything I can do to convince you to give me another chance?"

She was silent for a moment, giving him hope, then said, "I don't think so."

He ignored her response and continued his pitch. "Dinner? I—" He hesitated, then decided *what the hell.* May as well go full-on pathetic. "I received a job offer today, and I'm in the mood to celebrate. Maybe it's crazy, but for some reason I want to celebrate with you."

She held his gaze, and he could see he'd gotten to her. Her hazel eyes clouded and her lips tightened as she considered his words. Finally, she said, "Congratulations on the job offer, I hope it's a good fit and wish you the best of luck." She walked past him toward the closed door.

"Trina—"

She stopped, her back ramrod straight. He stepped up behind her, took in her warm, sultry scent.

"Thanks for the roses," she said, then opened the door and stepped into the hall.

Ψ

TRINA WAS SHAKING by the time she reached her cubicle. What had she done? Was she a fool for walking away from him, or had she just dodged a bullet?

All she knew was she felt nauseated. Like she'd made a huge mistake. But every time she thought about how he'd played her, she felt like such a fool. It was hard to let go of that. Hard to believe he wasn't secretly laughing at her. That he wouldn't mislead her again.

And yet, dammit, he *stirred* something in her. Kissing him had been insanely amazing. She'd been wound so tight after that, she couldn't sleep. And the way he'd followed her home, to ensure she was safe had been…wonderful, really.

She picked up the report she'd been working on, but there was no way she could focus on edits right now. She reached over to place it on the blasted file cabinet and was so distracted it took her a moment to realize the cabinet wasn't there. *Finally.*

Maintenance could be drilling out the locks right now. Just the distraction she needed—to find out what was in the top-secret file cabinet she'd been forced to live with for two years. Mara was probably in the conservation lab with Cressida and the cabinet, and she needed to let her know she was done using her office.

She found both women in the corridor, pushing the old reinforced beast down the hall on a hand truck. "Just wait. I bet it's going to be full of old health manuals," she said. "The ones they gave to sailors with warnings about VD."

Cressida snorted. "Just so long as it doesn't contain peen syringes, or other 'cures' for the clap. I do *not* want to catalogue used syringes."

Trina opened the door for the lab, and Cressida pushed the truck through while Mara held it steady.

"So, Trina, what happened with the SEAL?" Mara asked.

"He apologized for last night. And he wants to go out to dinner to celebrate his new job offer."

"That must be the one for Raptor. Alec mentioned it yesterday. Curt's going to have him vetted." She grinned. "Too bad I can't get that report for you. So where are you going to dinner?"

"I turned him down."

Cressida pushed the hand truck upright, and the file cabinet slammed to the floor. "You *what?*" she asked. "The guy is seriously yummy, and he apologizes like a champ. Flowers and an office visit. You said last night he didn't use any lame-ass qualifiers when he said he was sorry at the party. And he made sure you got home safely. Are you insane?"

Trina frowned. "Possibly."

She didn't even have to close her eyes to remember how he'd looked standing shirtless in his kitchen. Thick biceps on already broad shoulders, sculpted pecs, six-pack abs to die for. He had the body of an active-duty SEAL, the face of a model, and a vast library of books he organized using the Dewey decimal system.

"Oh, shit! I'm really stupid, aren't I?"

She bolted for the stairs, heading up to the ground floor. It was too late. She knew it was too late. He was long gone. But she had to try. She darted out of the building and jogged down the road for the nearest parking lot. This was ridiculous. She didn't even know if he'd driven to the Yard.

She scanned the lot for his Land Cruiser. It wasn't there.

Dammit. Why the hell did she have to have so much pride?

She returned to the building, to her cubicle. She didn't have his phone number but could probably get it through Mara. Or she could e-mail him.

She glanced at her watch. She was supposed to put in another hour today. She drummed her fingers on the desk.

After her cold treatment of him, she had to do more than send him an e-mail. He'd probably think she was e-mailing him about the Somalia op and delete it unopened—if he hadn't blocked her already.

She'd go to his place. If he wasn't home, she'd wait. She left Mara a voice mail, packed up her laptop and the report she'd been editing, and headed to the Metro. She could work on the train and while she waited in front of Keith's town house.

With every Metro stop, she reconsidered her decision.

What the hell was she afraid of? That a great guy who turned her on to an insane degree might actually be interested in her? Or that he was far too good, too cool, too perfect, for a woman like her?

Yeah, she had her insecurities. And it was time to let them go. Either they'd hit it off or they wouldn't. But she had to give him a chance.

By the time her train reached East Falls Church, she'd gotten a grip on her nerves. His town house was a quick walk from the station. Finally, at his door, she took a deep breath and rang the bell.

A minute passed. Two. She knocked again. Her heart pounded in time to the passing seconds. Her resolve to wait for him to get home flailed. She'd leave. Get his number from Mara and call him.

She turned just as the door opened and whirled to face him, her heart fluttering as she took in his unwelcoming expression.

"What the hell, Trina? It's not bad enough you handed me my ass at your office? You need to come to my home and kick me in the balls too? No, thanks." He stepped back and slammed the door.

The bang echoed in the quiet afternoon. Her face reddened. Okay, maybe *this* reaction was what she'd feared. But if he could grovel like a champ, so could she.

She rang the bell again. And again.

Finally, the door jerked open. "I will *never* answer your questions about Somalia. So unless you came over to watch me jack off, you need to leave."

She set her laptop bag in the doorway and grasped his shirt as she stepped up to bring them chest to chest. "I'm here to *help* you jack off."

His jaw settled into a firm line of distrust. "Are you for real? You seriously expect me to believe you changed your mind after the way you walked out at the Navy Yard?"

Her heart pounded. She couldn't believe she was being this forward, but dammit, she had nothing left to lose. "I don't expect you to believe it," she said, echoing his words from yesterday. "But it's true."

The tension in his jaw relaxed a titch.

She pressed closer to him and tightened her grip on his shirt. "I'm sorry, Keith. I'm a fool. I should have accepted your apology and dinner invitation. Can I have a do-over?"

He held her gaze for a long moment, then he slowly slid his hands around her waist and pressed her body against his, lifting her slightly as he lowered his head and kissed her.

She opened her mouth and welcomed his tongue. The kiss was hot, deep, and left no doubt it would lead upstairs and into his bedroom.

Keith broke the kiss. "You sure this is what you want, Trina?"

Her answer was a kiss, followed by more as she traced his jaw, enjoying the feel of the slight abrasion of afternoon stubble against her lips. She kissed downward, over his throat, down his neck, to the closed buttons on his shirt. She paused and undid the top button, then licked the bare skin revealed underneath.

Keith scooped her up with one arm, swiped her bag inside the enclosed stairwell with his foot, then closed the door and slid the dead bolt home with his free hand. He shifted her to his shoulder and climbed the stairs. Without pausing on the main floor, he crossed through the kitchen and living room, then climbed another flight. Finally, they arrived in his bedroom, and he stopped at the foot of his bed, where he slowly lowered her, her body sliding against the length of his until her feet hit the plush throw rug on the hardwood floor.

She spared a glance for his room—noting without surprise it was spotless. Nary a dust bunny in a bedroom that could grace the cover of a Pottery Barn for Men catalog, if there were such a thing.

His neat-freak tendencies were a decided turn-on, and she made a mental note to clean her apartment before inviting him over, because she had a feeling her habits would have the opposite effect on him.

This was crazy fast for Trina—she never jumped into bed with a guy this quickly—but it felt right. He felt right. For whatever reason, she wanted him, and hallelujah, he wanted her too.

She dispensed with the rest of the buttons on his shirt while he untucked her blouse and unfastened hers. Her mouth was on his in an unending hot kiss that spurred her to work faster at undressing him.

She reached for his belt and opened the buckle, and had moved to the button on his fly when a crashing boom split the air and rocked the town house. All at once, the floor beneath them shifted. Then it cracked, and a sudden fissure split the room. Keith shoved her backward onto his bed, as behind him the floor fell away.

CHAPTER SIX

KEITH COVERED TRINA, shielding her from the raining debris. His brain had gone straight to combat mode as he assessed threats. The front of the town house was three stories, starting with the garage, but it was built into a hillside, so the back, where his bedroom was, was only two stories above ground.

The blast must have been to the front... What the hell was it? It had sounded like an IED, but what could have triggered it?

More importantly, who and why?

The bedroom was still intact—for the most part. A fissure had split the room, and the hardwood floor on the other side of the break had collapsed. The interior wall slumped. A bad sign. A structural beam on the ground floor must have gone down.

No getting out through the bedroom door.

He didn't smell smoke—it must have been a quick flash. It took out the beam but hadn't caught fire...yet.

The gas line could have cracked. The garage would be filling with gas right now. Only a matter of time before the pilot light on the furnace would trigger a real explosion. No time to wait for rescue. He had to get Trina out of there. He ran his hands down her body, checking for injury. "You okay?"

His words were muted, as was her affirmative response. The boom had been loud enough to ring his bell and it would be minutes or even hours before hearing would return to normal.

He spoke directly into her ear. "We're going out through the back window. Quickly. Before the gas furnace goes."

Her eyes were wide with fear but, thankfully, not panic. They could panic together when they were safely on the ground and away from the town house. He prayed to hell his neighbors were evacuating their homes now.

He shifted his weight, slowly, carefully, just in case the room teetered on the brink of collapse. Pulling Trina with him, he crossed the short expanse of floor to the window. A narrow roof, cover for the back porch, jutted out two feet below the window. It should hold both their weight, as long as the joists hadn't cracked.

He swung his legs over the sill and tentatively placed his weight on the tar-paper shingles. The roof lurched. His weight could pull the whole thing down, but it might hold Trina. He straddled the sill and urged her to climb through.

She placed a foot on the roof, and nothing shifted. *Thank God.*

With his mouth next to her ear, he said, "Climb down the support post and run clear of the building. There's a gate in the back fence. Go through it, cross the road, and keep running. Don't look back. I'll follow. I promise."

She scooted across the roof. At the edge, she dropped flat to her belly, then slid her legs over the edge while gripping the gutter. She quickly shifted one hand to the corner post and dropped out of sight.

Keith waited until she ran clear of the roof before putting his weight on it, then he followed her lead and made his way to the edge. He slid on his butt, only flipping at the last moment to shove off the roof and jump backward. A support beam collapsed as he did so, and the roof came down, the debris falling with him to his small brick patio. He rolled to his feet and chased after Trina, catching her just on the other side of the gate. With an arm around her shoulders, he pushed her forward. They just needed to cross the lane and run up the rise, then they'd be far enough away—out of the blast zone.

But they didn't make it. A thunderous boom shook the ground. The shock wave sent him forward. He caught Trina and rolled, taking the brunt of the impact as he was ground into the paved road.

⟨Ψ⟩

TRINA COULDN'T BREATHE. She tried to suck in a breath, but nothing happened. Logically, she knew the impact had knocked the wind out of her, but it was hard to control the panic.

A high-pitched whine filled an otherwise silent void.

Can't breathe.

She rolled off Keith and struggled to her feet. He did the same. Massive road rash covered his arms. His back could only be worse.

The ground felt like it was still moving, but that was probably her battered equilibrium. She swayed. Tried to take in a breath. Nothing.

Keith cupped her face and said something. His mouth moved. Sound and air had both vanished, like she'd entered space but with a minimum of gravity.

A great, gasping groan sounded, breaking the noise and air vacuum. She'd made the sound and managed to take in a sliver of oxygen. Her lungs expanded, but not enough. Not nearly enough.

"Slowly, Trina." This from Keith. A muted sound that drifted below the buzz. "Don't try so hard." His shirt was open and hung from his arms in pieces. His belt was still undone. Blood dotted his arms and tattered clothes.

She managed another grunt, then a shallow breath. Slowly, her lungs filled with the acrid, smoke-filled air. She held her hand to her chest—her shirt was open like Keith's, but thankfully not shredded—and turned away from the burning crater to gasp for cleaner air.

With shaking hands, she buttoned her top. She had a million questions, but between her dulled hearing and inability to breathe, she could hardly voice them. Keith placed a hand on her back and pulled her close, hugging her against his chest.

She took in several slow breaths, utterly grateful for the feel of his beating heart against her cheek.

He spoke directly into her ear. "Ambulance, police, and fire will be here any moment. You need to be checked out at a hospital."

"So do you!" She yelled the words but could barely hear them.

He nodded. "I won't leave you." She read the words on his lips, heard them in a faint echo of sound that rode above the high-pitched ringing that tried to block everything else.

His lips touched hers, then he took her hand, and they slowly walked down the street, Trina with a slight limp. She'd twisted her ankle either when she climbed from the roof or when they rolled. She hadn't felt it at the time.

They had to circle a long block to get back to the street Keith's town house faced. Or rather, had faced. The wail of sirens cut through the ringing in her ears. The first responders were arriving.

They reached the corner and saw a crowd had formed a block ahead in front of the row of town houses. More people were filling the street as they approached. People's eyes widened and they cleared the way for them both as she limped toward a fire engine that blocked the wreckage that had been Keith's town house from view. Two firefighters were directing pedestrians to back off, creating a buffer between the people and the blast zone.

Trina scanned others in the crowd for signs of injury but saw none and hoped everyone had fled their townhomes after the initial blast, before the second, devastating one.

Depth of sound slowly returned, as if a filter had been removed. She heard both low murmurs from the onlookers and the high-pitched cry of a baby.

They rounded the tail of the fire engine to see the crater that had been his town house again. Debris still floated down. His house was on the end of the row. The adjacent home had also been destroyed. Only the far wall of the structure remained, sagging with jagged, crumbling edges.

Keith's gaze dropped. She squeezed his hand. "I'm sorry. So sorry."

"You're okay. I'm okay. As long as my neighbors are okay, I don't give a damn about my stuff."

A boy about eight years old shouted, "Keith!" and ran toward them with his arms out.

Keith dropped to his knees and hugged him. "Tyler, please tell me your family is okay." He ran his hand over the boy's dark curls.

"We're all fine. Even Patches is okay."

Trina looked up to see an African-American woman running toward them with a younger child in her arms and a dog on a leash. Keith let go of Tyler and hugged the woman. "Thank God."

She hugged him, but the toddler in her arms balked and squealed. The woman stepped back. "We got out right after the first blast. It shook the house, woke the baby. Tyler put Patches on a leash, and we bolted. Tyler wanted to go into your house to see if you were okay—" She caught her breath and spoke in a choked voice. "I couldn't let him."

Keith scooped the boy back into his arms. "Your mom was right. You're very brave, but never, ever go into a building after an explosion. Always do just what you did—grab your mom and your little brother, and get out. Fast. 'Kay?"

The boy nodded. "I wasn't scared." But his voice shook as he said it.

"It's okay to be scared, Ty. I was scared. And if your daddy had been home, he'd have been scared. Sometimes being scared is what keeps us safe, makes us stronger."

"You promised to teach me how to throw a football. Guess that won't happen now." Tyler glanced back at the burning wreckage, and Trina's heart went out to the little boy who'd just lost his home and was trying his best to figure out what it meant.

"I will," Keith said. "This weekend if I can. We'll take a video and send it to your daddy so he can give you pointers. He's a better player than me."

Tears burned Trina's eyes. The boy was handling the situation better than she was. Shock, fear, adrenaline, and now seeing Keith interact with this family—three people who could have died just moments ago—was almost her undoing.

First responders descended upon their small group, clearly alerted by their disheveled state. "Are you Keith Hatcher? Is that your home?"

Keith set Tyler down and nodded.

"Was there anyone else inside?"

"No. Just Trina and me." He put an arm around her and pulled her forward.

The questions began. First, she and Keith were put in the back of separate ambulances, and Falls Church police and a fire department investigator questioned her as a paramedic assessed her condition. Then the FBI arrived.

Except for scrapes, bruises, and a sore ankle, she was fine. She insisted on forgoing a trip to the hospital so she could be questioned on-site—and stay near Keith, who remained inside his ambulance long after she'd been released from medical care. She imagined a medic was cleaning the road rash on his back and arms.

In embarrassing detail, she described for the FBI everything that had happened. From arriving at Keith's house, his slamming the door in her face, to ending up in his bedroom. It was too early to determine where the initial blast had come from, but from eyewitness accounts of the state of the town house between the two explosions, they suspected the first had occurred at the front of the structure, on the lowest level.

Speculation ran in favor of the second, larger blast being caused by damage to the gas line from the first, but whether the initial one was an accident or deliberate was anyone's guess.

The fact that the FBI was involved so quickly was a sure sign that they were erring on the side of deliberate.

Which would mean someone had tried to kill Keith. But why?

Given his history with the Navy SEALs and the nature of the operations she knew he'd been on, there could be any number of reasons and suspects, but the FBI wasn't ready to rule out Trina as a potential target either. She was questioned extensively on her background and her high security clearance, and the fact that she worked for the attorney general's wife definitely caused some concern.

Mara, Erica, and Cressida arrived at some point while she was being questioned inside an FBI van. She had no clue how much time had passed, considering she was still in a hazy blur as the reality of what had happened slowly penetrated.

Full dark set in, and lights were strung up so investigation of the scene could continue unabated. Thunderstorm warnings meant investigators needed to collect as much data as they could before trace evidence would be washed away.

A headquarters of sorts had been set up at the perimeter, and Trina saw Keith only in passing as he crossed from the ambulance to a larger mobile crime scene investigation vehicle.

Curt arrived not long after her coworkers had, and there was a flurry amongst the FBI investigators. Not surprising considering it had to be rare for the AG to personally visit a potential crime scene. He made it clear he'd come out of friendship—but that didn't stop him from grilling her with the same intensity as the special agent in charge, who'd arrived only minutes before Curt.

A bomb going off in a former Navy SEAL's town house on the outskirts of the nation's capital brought out all the bigwigs.

She recounted her day to Curt and the SAC with the same degree of detail, including the fact that she'd borrowed Mara's office to talk to Keith at the Navy Yard. Who knew what was important at this point?

Done answering questions, she waited outside with her coworkers while Curt questioned Keith. Too tired to pace but too freaked-out to sit still, she stood and rubbed her arms, chilled in spite of it being an eighty-degree muggy summer night.

Finally, Keith stepped out of the mobile unit. Cressida, Mara, and Erica all faded into the background as he made a beeline for her. His arms came around her, and she pressed against him, feeling like she could finally breathe again after having the wind knocked out of her hours ago.

He held her for a long time, stroking her back. She simply breathed and melted into him, holding him for all she was worth.

It had to end eventually, she supposed. Keith's arms loosened, then he kissed her lightly on the lips. He stroked her hair. "You look exhausted."

"I am. You, on the other hand, look fine. I find that unfair."

"Training. This wasn't my first unexpected explosion." He frowned. "But it was the first in the US that threatened civilians." He sighed. "Listen, Trina, I called Rav. Much as I want to be with you, I'm going to stay at one of the Raptor facilities while we get this sorted out."

If there was one thing Trina needed right now, it was to be with Keith. Not for sex, but just to hold him and be held. They'd just been through something together, and maybe it wasn't rational, but he was the only person she wanted to be with in the aftermath. "Fine. I'll go with you."

"No. Until we know what's going on, I'm a danger to you."

"What if *I'm* the reason the bomb was set? For all we know, I'm endangering *you.*"

"What reason could anyone possibly have to try to kill you? The people you write about are all dead."

"Not all of them. You're still alive."

"Yeah, but we've established that you aren't studying me." He frowned. "I'm a former SEAL. I've been on a lot of ops." He hesitated for a moment, then added, "I've killed people. There are reasons certain people could want me dead. Until we know who, I refuse to endanger you—or anyone." He swore and rubbed his hand across his face. "I still need to figure out how I'm going to tell Tyler I can't play ball with him. I never should have promised. I didn't know what else to say."

It was clear Keith was resolute, and no amount of argument would convince him. And what if he was right? What if this had been a deliberate attack, revenge for the orders he'd carried out while in the Navy?

She, of all people, knew history. She knew what clandestine operations entailed. She didn't know the details of his particular ops, but she had highly educated insight into the nature of his work. "Will you call me?"

He shook his head. "No. No contact until this is sorted out. Period."

She crossed her arms. "You still owe me dinner."

He laughed. "Babe, I promise, as soon as we know it's safe, you can pick the restaurant. Hell, I'll fly you to Paris if you want."

"I prefer Italy."

He hooked both index fingers in her belt loops and tugged her forward. His kiss was hard, fierce. A sexy, sweet, sad good-bye. "Just promise you'll wait for me, and you've got a deal."

Chapter Seven

(Ψ)

"YOU CAN'T EVEN keep your nose clean for six hours," Rav said when he arrived at the scene.

Keith grimaced. "You never said I had to keep my nose clean. You just said there'd be a proctology exam."

"Well, I figured you knew you'd have to *pass* it." Then Rav smiled and held out his hand. They clasped wrists, and Rav gave him a one-armed hug with a pat on the back. "Shit, Hatch. This sort of thing isn't supposed to happen at home."

Keith nodded and rubbed his forehead. "The family next door lost their house. They all could have died. Trina could have died. All my years in the Navy, and I've never been so scared."

Trina's coworkers had taken her home. It was just Rav, Dominick, and Keith standing in the shadows—*never stand in the light when you're a target*—on the edge of the makeshift HQ. It looked freakily like a field HQ in a war zone. Except this was two hundred yards from his *home*. Or rather, where his home used to be.

Thunder rent the air, and the storm finally made good on its promise. Fat drops came slowly at first, but within minutes, it became a downpour. Keith didn't budge; he just stood letting the rain wash the blast dust from his clothes. He'd buttoned up his torn shirt after the medic had tweezed gravel and glass from his back and arms. For all the good it did him, the destroyed shirt and scuffed jeans were the only clothes he had. The only *anything* he had.

Absolutely everything he owned had been in the town house, including his Land Cruiser, which had been parked in the garage.

He turned to the two men. The pity party would happen later. "What security do you have for Trina?"

"She should be okay at work," Curt said. "Marines provide security on the base, which is particularly tight these days, but I've already called and requested armed marines be stationed inside her building."

Keith nodded. "Good. As soon as the press releases her name, she'll be a target. The bomber will think she's important to me." And she was important to him, which was a little crazy when he considered that he'd only met her yesterday morning. He looked at Rav. "What can you do about security for her outside the Navy Yard?"

"One of my operatives is guarding her apartment already. He'll be assigned to her whenever she's not at work, but she'll need to cooperate and call him to escort her when she leaves."

"She's smart. She'll cooperate. Private security will be pricey; I'll pay Raptor every cent of the cost."

Rav shook his head. "I can afford it. Consider it an advance on your salary if it bothers you."

Keith didn't really give a crap about the details. He just wanted to know Trina was protected.

ψ

TWO DAYS AFTER the explosion, Trina returned to work. The aches from the tumble on the pavement had only just started to ease, but she'd been ready to lose her mind pacing her apartment, her only company a Raptor operative named Sean Logan who was nice and funny, but who wasn't Keith.

And wasn't it crazy that she longed to be with a man she barely knew?

Her laptop had been destroyed in the blast, so most of her first day back was spent dealing with getting a replacement, and the rest of the week was spent configuring it and uploading the backup files from the network server.

She worked through the weekend to get caught up due to the lost week, and now, a full week after the explosion she was back in her cubicle with first-person accounts of naval operations strewn across her desk and analysis of the successes and failures of SEAL Team 4 in Operation Just Cause—the 1989 invasion of Panama— to write.

She should feel normal again. After all, she'd only lost her wallet, cell phone, laptop, and a book in the blast. Nothing that couldn't be replaced. Every time she considered how much Keith and the family next door had lost, she had to choke back tears.

Keith's library. Tyler's baby pictures. Everything gone in an instant.

"You should go home," Mara said.

She startled and realized she'd been staring off into space. Mara leaned against the opening of her cubicle partition, and Trina had no idea how long she'd been there. "Maybe I should. But I feel like I'm going crazy there. All I can do is pace."

"Let's leave, then. It's almost five anyway. We can go to the mall at Pentagon City. You really need to get a new cell phone. While we're there, you can try on shoes."

Trina's jaw dropped. Mara hated shopping only slightly less than Erica did. Offering Trina one of her favorite pastimes—shoe shopping—was about the sweetest gesture she could imagine. But the crazy thing was, the idea of shoe shopping didn't appeal.

What she wanted was to see Keith, which she figured was even nuttier than not wanting to find the right pair of stilettos to go with that little purple dress she had no reason to wear. "I don't know. We'd have to drag the Raptor bodyguard with us."

Mara frowned. "How long has he worked for the company?"

"He told me Alec hired him six months ago."

"He'll do, then." Mara didn't trust anyone who'd worked for the company under the previous owner, and Trina didn't blame her for that. "Call him and tell him to pick us up."

"Okay, but we're not going shoe shopping. I have more shoes than any woman needs. But I know a boy who needs a football."

ψ

THE MALL WAS located right on a Metro line and was a popular place during commuter hours. Trina picked up a new cell phone and replaced her laptop bag before they went to a toy store to buy a football for Tyler.

She'd learned more about the family's situation in the week following the explosion. Tyler's dad was in the Army and serving a tour overseas, what they hoped would be his last as troops were withdrawn from Afghanistan. With the family home destroyed, strings were being pulled to bring the father home, but it would be at least another week before that would be accomplished.

After finding a football suitable for small hands, Trina went a little overboard and bought the boy several other items, including a Razor scooter, a basketball, and Nerf dart shooters that might not be the most politically correct toy, but, according to her similarly aged nephews and nieces, were really fun. If Tyler's mother didn't approve, she'd donate them to Toys for Tots during the holidays.

Toy shopping done, they found themselves in a clothing store, where Mara bought a few blouses for work. Trina browsed skirts and sundresses, but her heart wasn't in it.

"Wow. *I'm* buying clothes and you're not? You sure you're not feverish?" Mara was probably the only person who could tease her, considering she'd been through an ordeal much more nightmarish than the explosion. She'd faced a firing squad in North Korea, after all.

Trina shrugged. "I just blew my budget on a new cell phone and toys."

"Good point. If you're not interested in shopping, let's get a drink."

Trina mustered a smile. "It *is* margarita weather."

"They have a nice lounge at the Ritz, and it's quieter than the mall restaurants."

She'd never been in the Ritz Carlton attached to the mall; both the hotel and restaurant were far too pricey for her budget, but she figured she'd earned a treat. As he'd done during their entire shopping venture, Sean the bodyguard followed them at a discreet distance. Inside, they were seated at a small table, while Sean sat at the bar.

Their drinks had barely been delivered when Mara stood and dropped money on the table. She leaned close to Trina, pressing one hand on the table, and lowered her voice to a whisper. "Stay here until Sean and I leave, then cut through the lobby to the elevator." She grabbed her shopping bag, hitched her purse over her shoulder, and said in a normal tone, "Ladies room. Be right back."

Trina stared at her, feeling clueless, then reached for her drink. Her eyes fell on the card that must have been under Mara's hand on the table. Trina lifted the plastic Ritz Carlton hotel room key card, noting the room number indicated on the sticky note, and tucked it in her purse. Minutes later, Mara reentered the lounge, now wearing one of her new blouses—which happened to be the same coral color as the blouse Trina wore. More significant, however, was the fact that Mara wore glasses and her hair was now dark and pulled back in a knot similar to the one at the nape of Trina's neck.

A wig?

Sean's gaze flicked to Trina, then he stood and followed Mara across the lounge, through the lobby and, Trina could only assume, into the mall.

Mara was slightly shorter and far curvier than Trina, but with the wig and wearing the right colored top in a loose fit, a casual observer could easily think Trina was leaving the mall with Sean.

She took a sip of her drink, utterly flummoxed. Mara must have been carrying the wig and glasses in her purse the whole time. And she'd ever so casually purchased the top, which really should have clued Trina in, considering how little Mara liked trying on clothes. Hell, she should have guessed something was up when the woman had offered to go clothes shopping in the first place.

She took one last swallow of margarita, then stood. With a rapidly beating heart, she gathered her shopping bags and headed to the lobby, where she went straight to the bank of elevators.

Time stretched in opposite proportion to the pounding in her chest. Surely it was the longest elevator ride of her life. Finally, a bell rang and the doors slid open. A moment later, she slid the card into the slot, and the lock light turned green.

She pushed open the door and came face-to-face with Keith.

CHAPTER EIGHT

KEITH'S BREATH CAUGHT to see beautiful, gorgeous, sexy Trina in the entry hall. Hands filled with bulging shopping bags, she stood with her hip cocked and uncertainty in her gaze. He wanted to step forward and take her into his arms, but this was Trina's move. He'd arranged this without her knowledge. He wouldn't touch her until he was certain she wanted him to.

"Damn you." Her mouth was tight, her words clipped.

Shit. This had been a mistake. She was pissed. They were eternally out of sync. One of them was always waltzing while the other moved to a hip-hop beat. Their discordant notes would never mesh.

She dropped the bags, kicked the door closed, and stepped forward. "If I'd known I was going to see you, I'd have worn my purple dress. Or sexier underwear."

The foolish panic evaporated. They were dancing to the same tune after all. "I don't care what your underwear looks like, because I'm sort of hoping you won't be wearing it long."

"Works for me." She untucked her blouse, then pulled it over her head without unbuttoning, tossing it to the side.

Keith figured that was a positive indication she wanted him to touch her. He stepped forward and cupped her cheeks—instead of going straight for her breasts like he really wanted to do. "I've missed you like crazy." Then he tasted her. Strawberries. Sweet. Hot. Perfect.

She fumbled with the buttons on his shirt, managing to open the top two, then he followed her lead and lifted it over his head and tossed it aside. He pulled her against him, and at last they were skin to skin. Except for the bra, which had to go. But before he could remove it, she nudged him backward, deeper into the suite, then paused, taking in the surroundings. "You got a suite?"

He nodded. "More room for pacing while waiting."

"How long have you been here? All week?"

"No. I'm staying in a safe house. I was pacing while waiting for you. Sean needed to be certain you hadn't been followed before he'd give the go-ahead. Rav insisted on someone pretending to be you, just in case you were being watched from an undetected source."

"I would imagine Curt wasn't thrilled with Mara playing decoy."

"She volunteered, but I have a feeling she didn't tell him."

Trina suppressed a smile with tight lips. "We're asking for trouble in pissing off the head of the Justice Department like that."

"Hopefully Mara will be able to defuse him before he comes after me. Cressida and Erica offered too, but they're both too tall."

"You mean every one of my coworkers knew I was going to see you today, while I was left in the dark?"

He dropped light kisses along her jaw. "If Sean had spotted a tail, this would have been called off. Mara was concerned you'd argue if that happened. Plus, I think she enjoyed springing this on you."

Those beautiful lips curved into a sexy smile. "She really fooled me. She even asked about Sean, as if she had no idea who was guarding me. But I'm not complaining. It was a great surprise. Now, are you going to get naked or not?"

"Ladies first."

She laughed, then glanced around. "Is it strange that I'm nervous? I mean, the last time we got to this point, the world went boom."

"We can take this as slow as you want. We don't have to make love. The room comes with HBO. *Game of Thrones* is on."

Her laugh was sharp as she grabbed his belt and pulled him toward her. "Don't think you're getting off that easy—or rather, not getting off—I'm not leaving here until you've rocked my world." She'd dispensed with the buckle before she finished speaking.

He grinned. "Good, because *Game of Thrones* is a repeat." He bit her shoulder gently, then nipped along the crest to the base of her neck. She smelled so good—a scent that was flowery, clean, feminine. Sexy as hell. Trina through and through. "And I really want to be inside you."

She tugged down his zipper. "I can make that happen." She

dropped to her knees, and before he caught his breath, he was inside her mouth. She opened her throat and took him deep.

"Babe—" He lost the ability to speak as she stroked her tongue up the base of his cock, then tightened her lips for a fast slide down the shaft, again taking him all the way to the back of her throat. Trina's sweet, hot mouth on his cock, the way she barely grazed the tip with her teeth, then slid and sucked was intense. And God, the way she looked, with those sexy glasses perched on her perfect nose as his cock disappeared into her mouth. This was every fantasy he'd had in the last lonely week, times ten.

Her hand wrapped around the base of his cock, and she stroked in time with lips and tongue. The sensation was enough to bring him to the edge, so he pulled back, sliding from her hot mouth.

There was no way he was going to let her get him off so soon. He had his own tasting and exploring to do. "Babe, get naked and get on the bed."

She kicked off her shoes as he did the same. He doffed his jeans and briefs, then helped her with her slacks. Once she was stripped of all but her bra and panties, he scooped her up, crossed to the bedroom, and deposited her on the bed.

He stood back and let his gaze feast on her. She was slender and fit. Flat belly, smooth skin. Her hands covered her beige bra, hiding her shape from view. He met her gaze and shook his head. "I want to see all of you, Trina." He settled on the bed next to her and lifted one of her hands. "Every delicious inch." He kissed the inside of her wrist. "You are beautiful. Perfect."

"I'm not exactly busty."

He undid the clasp of her bra and removed the small scrap of fabric, then he took one nipple into his mouth as he stroked the other breast. He lifted his head to meet her gaze. "Perfect." He read the doubt in her eyes and realized she was more self-conscious than she wanted him to know. He took her hand and placed it on his erection. "Babe, this is how I react to your body. I couldn't be more turned on if you were a D-cup. Your breasts are gorgeous and *you*. Anything more wouldn't be you." He grazed a nipple with his teeth, then sucked it into his mouth. "And if you want, I'll spend all night showing your breasts exactly how much I appreciate them."

She smiled then, all traces of insecurity gone, the confident sexy woman he'd been fantasizing about for a week back in charge. She pushed at his chest, forcing him onto his back. "You're the one who is perfect. My God. Do you work out six hours a day?"

He laughed as her hands explored his chest, the look on her face making every painful minute in the gym worthwhile. "Not *that* much. At least, not since I joined the Navy—the whole first year was one long, brutal workout." She licked an ab, and her tongue trailed south. "Oh, no you don't, babe. It's my turn."

A quick shift had her on her back with him leaning over her. He flicked his tongue across one nipple, then the other, sucking on the point, loving the feel of the pert tip on his tongue.

He moved lower, kissing her belly, nipping and nibbling until he came to the juncture of her thighs. He pulled off her underwear, then spread her legs and passed his thumb across her clitoris. She bucked as if receiving an electrical jolt. He smiled and stroked her clit again. Again, she twitched and this time let out a soft pant. He leaned closer to take in her aroused scent.

He didn't think it was possible, but his erection reached new heights.

He spread her lips. She was wet and ready, but he wasn't about to rush this. He licked her clit, then slid his tongue inside her, thrusting deep. His thumb found her clit again and rubbed in time with his tongue. Her thighs clenched against him, and she gasped, a full-body reaction that transferred to him like an electrical current.

Trina turned him on and lit him up like no other. He'd decided to stop asking himself why and just enjoy. And right now he was seriously enjoying the way she felt against his tongue. And he loved the way she threaded her fingers through his hair as her thighs clenched. Intensity built, and she pulled back, only to push against him a second later, craving his touch as much as he needed to taste her.

He brought her close to the edge with his mouth, then pressed his fingers to her clit, holding her there. He slid up her body and kissed her, hard and deep, all while his fingers applied steady pressure.

She reached for his cock as she sucked on his tongue. She soon found a rhythm that kept him in the same state of unending arousal. "I'm not on any kind of birth control. And I don't think

I've ever regretted that decision so much as right this moment."

"You think I'd lure you to the Ritz and forget the condoms? That would be like planning an op but forgetting to bring bullets."

She laughed. "Where?"

"Nightstand drawer."

She released him and crawled across the king-size bed. Her ass looked amazing as she bent over the drawer to grab the box.

She returned with a condom, pushed him onto his back again, and tore open the packet. But she surprised him and took him into her mouth and sucked all the way down before releasing him and rolling the condom over his erection.

Once he was sheathed, she straddled him and took him inside, slowly descending until he was seated to the hilt.

She felt fucking amazing. And the way she panted and mewed as he filled her only added to the intensity. She leaned forward, bringing them skin to skin—her soft, flat belly to his abs, her nipples brushed against his chest—as his cock thickened even more inside her.

He placed his hands on her hips and thrust from below, holding her for a slow, sensuous slide as his cock stroked her inside. She kissed him as she rode him, her tongue doing to him what his cock did to her.

He shifted his hands to her cheeks, releasing her mouth so he could look in her eyes. "Babe, I can't touch your clit unless you sit up. Do you need—?"

She shook her head and gasped. "No. I'm there." And then she arched her back and let out the sexiest breathy sound he'd ever heard. Her body quaked. She didn't stop rocking her hips against his, even as her orgasm continued. The hot friction of his thrusts combined with the electric-like jolts of her body pushed him over the edge, and pleasure ripped through him in a sharp, intense torrent.

She gasped and collapsed against him. "Holy hell, that was amazing."

He chuckled, causing her to bounce on his chest. "Agreed."

"I suppose I should have taken my glasses off, but I wanted to see you." She ran a hand across his chest and down his abs, tracing the indentations between muscles, as if his body were a maze to be solved.

"I frigging love your glasses. Leave them on. Always." He

tugged at her bun, which had loosened as they made love. "I sort of have a thing for your sexy-librarian look."

She laughed. "It's not a look—it's just easier to wear my hair up, and I've never liked contact lenses."

He nibbled on her neck, his heart still slowing, loving everything about holding her and feeling a contentment that was new to him.

She shifted, and he slid out of her. He disposed of the condom, then gathered her against him.

"How long do we have?" she asked.

"If you want, Sean can pick you up and deliver you to work in the morning. Cressida sent over an overnight bag—in case you decided to stay."

She cupped his cheeks. "I want to stay."

He kissed her. "We'll order room service for dinner."

"Sounds perfect."

Keith made the order, then they lay in bed, touching and talking, avoiding serious subjects like bombs and destroyed homes and top-secret Navy ops. She told him about her family—she was the middle child of three girls and moved to DC from Ohio for graduate school—and he indicated that he had a family but didn't offer more.

"I know you went straight from high school to the Navy. Did you always want to be a SEAL?"

He paused. Her question came dangerously close to one subject he wanted to avoid—his father. But if this were going to develop into something more than a tryst in an expensive hotel, he'd have to share his past. And he *did* want more with Trina. For the first time in his life, he didn't have to worry about leaving someone behind when he was deployed. He didn't have to settle for a superficial relationship.

"No. I wanted to be quarterback for the San Francisco 49ers. I even had a full-ride scholarship to Notre Dame—just like Joe Montana."

"But you went into the Navy instead. Why didn't you go to the Academy in Annapolis, where you could have played football?"

"It was too late to apply to the Academy when I joined." He pulled her close to his side and tucked a loose strand of her hair behind her ear. "I attended Notre Dame for all of two weeks and played in one college football game. I was a true freshman, backup

QB. Opening game of the season and we were losing—badly. I was sent in at the very end. I threw two passes—both completed—but I was also sacked twice. We lost. Three days later, September eleventh happened."

He paused. Trina, a military historian, might understand how that day had changed him, but few people in his life then had. His girlfriend at the time hadn't gotten it. Some teammates hadn't understood. His dad certainly didn't.

His dad *still* didn't get it.

He hoped to hell Trina would understand.

"Dreams of being Joe Montana didn't sit well with you after that, did they? You were, what? Eighteen? Physically fit if you were playing college ball, and you had nothing holding you back. Someone had to go to Afghanistan and find bin Laden."

He pulled her tightly against him, unable to mask the surge of emotion. "Yes. Everything I'd dreamed before that day felt hollow. There was a Navy man in me all along. I just hadn't known it." Here, he came close to the sensitive subject, but telling her felt right. "The military had never been an option when I was growing up—my dad was adamantly opposed, pretty much antigovernment in whatever form.

"My teammates, some of them understood. Others felt like I was judging them for not stepping forward, like I thought football was worthless and if they chose a sport over service, they were shallow. But I was doing what *I* needed to do, what felt right for me. There was no judgment. And, hell, I still love football." He stroked her back. "I quit school that week and joined the Navy. I've never regretted it."

"I'm curious. Why the Navy? Afghanistan is landlocked."

"That decision was for the SEALs. My goal from the first moment I joined was to get into the SEALs."

She touched the healing cuts on his shoulders and arms, the last remnants of the explosion they'd survived. "Why did you leave?"

"I'd served. I decided it was time to have a life. Plus I have a friend who is going through some stuff…health issues…and I wanted to be nearby. I left the Navy three months ago. When you've lived on adrenaline for years, it's hard to come down, so I was taking a break before looking for work. I'd considered using the GI bill to start school in September, but now Rav has offered

me a job. Something better than anything I'd be offered even with
a college degree."

"Do you think the explosion has something to do with the
job?"

"It's more likely it has to do with the SEALs." His heart kicked
up again. "Trina, I assume you know what I did for the SEALs."

She nodded. "I've read your service file. You were a sniper."

He let out the breath he'd been holding. "You're okay with
that?"

"Of course. I know one well-placed bullet can save a thousand
lives."

Sometimes the number can be as high as five thousand.

Given her background and the firmness of her words, he
believed she meant it. He could fall in love with this woman, and
crazily enough, the idea didn't seem...crazy. A knock on the door
stopped him from saying something foolish. He kissed her lightly
on the lips, then got up and threw on jeans while she ducked into
the bathroom.

Minutes later, room service delivered, she joined him, wearing
a plush hotel robe, and sat next to him at the small table.

She took a sip of her wine, then asked, "So how long do we
play hide-and-seek and meet only for covert trysts?"

"We won't do this again. If someone was following you, it
won't work twice. I only decided it was worth the risk because
there's been no sign you're being monitored at all. But that could
change, and I don't want anyone realizing you're important to me,
and coming after you." He'd just admitted she was important to
him—probably too soon, but like joining the Navy, something he
refused to regret.

Her gaze held an intensity that she left unvoiced. She cleared
her throat. "So... What are we going to do?"

"I haven't figured that out yet." He set down his fork. "I'm
hoping you'll be willing to wait. At least until we know more."

"Of course." She paused. "I'm not ready to put a name to
this"—she swept out her hand to indicate her robe, him, the
ornate hotel room—"but I know it—*you*—are worth waiting for."

He'd heard those words before—once he'd even wanted to
hear them—but this was the first time he both wanted the words
and believed them.

CHAPTER NINE

TRINA COULDN'T CONCENTRATE on work Tuesday morning. Her mother would say she was twitterpated. And she'd be right.

The night with Keith had been nothing short of amazing. Just thinking about how he'd arranged it took her breath away. Memories of the sex was enough to make her combust, but thoughts of the connection behind it made her knees weak. In her experience, hot, perfect men like Keith eschewed relationships for flings with women who were taller, prettier, and bustier than she was, but he clearly wanted her—repeatedly, in fact—and there had been more going on than two people getting off together.

She could fall head over heels for him and wasn't even freaked out by the idea. Truth was, it might already have happened, but it was too soon to even consider the L-word.

It was still early in the morning when Mara looked over the cubicle wall in her best Kilroy impersonation, sparking the idea of writing a paper on the significance of Kilroy graffiti to the war effort during World War II. But unlike the cartoon figure, Mara had a Cheshire cat grin. And Trina couldn't help but return it.

"Sorry I had to bail last night," Mara said without an ounce of sorrow in her tone.

Trina responded with her own grin. "I forgive you."

"I figured you might," Mara said, then continued down the corridor.

Trina gathered a notebook and digital recorder. She had to interview Walt's Desert Storm vet, a former Navy aviator. Walt had originally scheduled the interview for last Tuesday, the day after the explosion, but she wasn't fit for work. When she didn't show for the interview, Walt took it upon himself to reschedule, and Trina didn't have the energy to fight him on it when she returned to work. Now it was too late to back out.

Instead of taking the Metro, Sean gave her a ride to the coffee shop near Union Station. There was something to be said for having a permanent bodyguard with a car. Plus he was a nice guy, good-looking—his ebony skin, big muscles, and a great smile reminded her of the football player Russell Wilson in looks and physique—and good company when she wanted someone to talk to but also unobtrusive when she wanted to pretend she didn't have a babysitter.

Sean sat two tables away in the crowded coffee shop and gave no indication they were together. Trina settled into a seat across from Lieutenant Brian Ruby, noticing right away that his body language was all wrong. He was hostile or agitated. He kept his head down, barely acknowledging her when she introduced herself.

With a frown, she set her digital recorder on the table between them and hit Record. May as well begin. "Lieutenant," she said, "in late fall of 1991, you were transferred to a temporary assignment with a UN peacekeeping force, a post-Desert Storm coalition. According to my colleague's notes, you left that six-month assignment after only three weeks. The record is scant at best. Can you tell me why you left before completing the assignment?"

She had walked into this interview with less background information than she liked. Walt had given her the man's service files last week, but they'd been incomplete. Distracted by replacing her lost computer files, she had forgotten to follow up on the missing documents and had foolishly entered this interview cold, with little more than starting questions drafted by Walt.

Ruby leaned forward. His gaze darted around the room, then he said loudly, "Blow me, and I'll tell you everything."

Trina bolted to her feet, her face flushing as she caught the startled stares from the couple at the next table. "Lieutenant," she said through clenched teeth, "this interview is being recorded. You aren't doing yourself any favors."

"Listen, honey, I'm just asking for the same service you give your other interviewees. Did Hatcher tell you everything you wanted to know?"

Her stomach went cold. Her name had been in the news with Keith's after the explosion, and Keith had insisted the official press release state she was there to interview him, to prevent anyone who was after him from thinking she was important to him. But any number of Falls Church officers and FBI agents knew the truth. They'd both been honest about where they were and what they were doing at the time of the first explosion. Which meant either someone had talked or Lieutenant Ruby had tossed out the accusation simply to offend her. Neither option sat well. She plucked her digital recorder from the table and grabbed her purse.

Ruby glanced around the shop again and raised his lip in a sneer. "What's wrong, honey? You don't want word to get out that you'll fuck for information? I suppose that could be a problem for you. Then you might have to blow the older guys too, not just the young SEALs."

A hand on her arm gently nudged her aside. She turned, almost expecting to see Keith, but her champion was Sean, who planted his hands on the table and leaned into Ruby's face. "Apologize to Dr. Sorensen."

"Are you the guy she's fucking now?" He met Trina's gaze. "You sure do get around."

Sean grasped the front of the lieutenant's shirt and yanked him to his feet as Trina rocked back on her heels. "Apologize to the lady." Sean's voice was low, carrying more than a hint of menace.

"Lady, my ass. She's just another whore and a government hack. I'm sick of bitches like her."

Sonofabitch. What the hell had Walt set her up for?

The tables around them cleared. One woman appeared to be calling 911. Not your typical morning at Starbucks. "Let him go, Sean. He's not worth it." She'd been saying that a lot lately.

He sighed. "I know. But, damn, it would be so satisfying." He released Ruby, and the man dropped into his seat. Ruby, a former naval officer and only about ten years older than Sean, was no slouch, but he was still no match for the Raptor operative in his prime.

Back in Sean's car, Trina buckled her seat belt and flopped back into the seat. "I wish I knew what just happened there."

"What was the interview supposed to be about?"

"Walt's questions were about UN Security Forces post-Desert Storm."

Sean pulled out his cell phone and hit a speed dial button. After a moment, he said, "Keith, something strange just happened... No. Trina is fine. She's right next to me. She was just interviewing a dickhead pilot who"—he looked apologetically at

Trina—"implied she had sex with you to get you to talk."

"He more than implied," Trina said, loud enough for Keith to hear. She had to admit, she was jealous Sean was able to call Keith. She didn't even have his phone number.

"My gut says there's more going on here. The guy was a dick, sure, but he came spoiling for a fight and armed with your name." Sean paused. "Will do." Then he hit the End button and tucked his phone away. He put his car in gear and pulled into traffic.

"Where are we going?"

"To your office. We need to talk to Walt."

⚓

KEITH WATCHED LIEUTENANT Ruby with a riflescope from a vantage point nearly a block away from the man's apartment in the Anacostia neighborhood. The man arrived home minutes after Keith took his position. He appeared twitchy, ready to bolt. Keith would bet good money his bag was packed; he was just waiting for his moment.

He needed to know why this bastard had insulted Trina, and why he had mentioned Keith specifically.

Ruby looked furtively out the window, and Keith wondered if he had gone soft or if he was just stupid. Backlit behind thin curtains, he might as well have painted a target on his face.

Keith plucked out his phone and dialed. "Something stinks about this, Rav. Ruby is a tool."

"After work, Sean is going to bring Trina here. Her roommate Cressida too. I don't like the security at her place, and I'm starting to wonder if this could be about her, not you."

"A safe house is a better idea. You're knee-deep in a campaign. Too many people coming and going."

"She can't join you, Keith. Not until we determine who the intended target is."

Keith held back a sigh. "I know that. I meant a different safe house."

"I'll see what I can arrange."

Down the street, Ruby checked the roadway in front of his apartment again. "I think Ruby is going to rabbit."

"I'm sending an operative to take over surveillance. I don't like you leaving the safe house. Give me thirty minutes."

"I can take care of myself. I used a surveillance detection route.

No one followed me."

"The point of a safe house is to hide."

Keith grimaced. "I was going insane hiding."

"Then go back to the Virginia compound and use the shooting range again."

He'd spent two days at the compound last week, sighting in a new M110 rifle and Sig handgun, replacements for the ones he'd lost in the blast. He'd blown through hundreds of rounds to fight the frustration of knowing there'd been zero progress in the investigation of the explosion. The idea of more target shooting held no appeal. "No, thanks."

"After your replacement gets there, come in to the office. Lee is coming in to map out the computer issues at the Alaska compound. We can bring you up to speed on the issues at the same time."

"Fine." Keith hung up and watched. Waited, all the while feeling uneasy. Anxious. At least going in to Rav's office would give him something to do. Ten minutes passed, then his phone vibrated. Hopefully Sean had located Walt Fryer.

No such luck. His caller was Josh Warner, a member of his SEAL team, and one of the few men who was more family to Keith than his biological brothers. He'd considered moving back to the San Francisco Bay Area when he left the service, but after his visit with his dad, he'd accepted that there was no reason to call California home anymore, and in fact, keeping the width of the continent between him and his father could only be a good thing. So he'd settled in Falls Church, and the fact that Josh lived in the DC area played a role in that choice.

"We've got a problem," Josh said.

Keith was more alarmed by Josh's tone than his words. After serving in the SEALs together, the problems they'd faced had ranged from a crappy dinner in the mess hall to calling for air support because insurgents had them pinned. Josh's tone said this wasn't a mess-hall sort of problem. "What's going on?"

"The rehab center just called me. Owen left."

Keith swore. "And they let him?"

"They couldn't stop him. He's voluntary."

"But they were supposed to call you before it gets to that point—"

"Someone screwed up, that's for sure. But the administrator

said everything was going fine. Owen was doing fine. Participating. He was one of the model patients. Then he got a phone call and just…flipped out."

Dread snaked up Keith's spine. "Who called him?"

"That's the strangest part. No one knows. Whoever it was, they knew the password, so the rehab center let Owen take the call."

"Shit." Only a very small list of people knew the code word, but unfortunately, Owen's aunt—who had medical power of attorney over the former SEAL so she had to be kept in the loop—was one of them. She was a sweet woman, with the best of intentions and only love for her broken nephew, but she also had no clue what could be at stake, and if convinced it would help Owen, she'd give up the password. He felt nauseated, but he had to ask, "Was the caller a woman?"

"You're thinking of the historian who contacted all of us? I thought you and she were on better terms after the explosion, and that she knows none of us will talk about Somalia."

If the situation didn't suck so badly, he'd smile at the phrase "better terms." He adjusted his scope when he caught another glimpse of Ruby in the window. "We're on very good terms. But I still have to ask, was the caller a woman?"

"Yes—at least the nurse thinks so."

That doesn't mean it was Trina.

"Did he say where he was going?" Keith asked.

"No. I'm going to head north and question the staff in person. I'll let you know if I hear anything. Can you stake out his aunt's house?"

Keith closed his eyes. Any other time, Owen would be his first priority. Shit, the one time one of his SEAL brothers *wasn't* his first priority, look what happened to Owen. If Keith hadn't needed to cover his own ass, Owen wouldn't be in the mess he was in now. Guilt or no guilt, Keith couldn't watch over Owen. Not today. "I've got a bit of a situation myself. And it involves the historian and possibly the explosion."

Thankfully, Josh didn't judge him—at least not out loud. "The explosion takes priority."

"I'll call Rav and see if he can send someone to the aunt's house. Call me if you find out anything from the rehab staff."

"Will do. Stay safe, man."

Keith hung up, and almost immediately, his phone rang again. Expecting Josh had forgotten something, he was surprised to see the caller identified as Curt Dominick, and forced a shift in mental gears. He was worried about Owen, but right now he had other problems.

He and Dominick had exchanged numbers, but the big man had yet to call Keith—a relief since Dominick's wife had volunteered for decoy duty yesterday, and odds were he would happily nail Keith to the wall for that. And he couldn't blame the guy. He kept his scope fixed on Ruby's window as he answered.

"I just received the forensic report on the initial blast. Wherever Trina is, get her out of there. Move her to your safe house. Now."

Adrenaline surged through Keith. "She's at the Navy Yard."

Curt swore.

Keith cleared his throat, trying to speak around the lump lodged there. "Why?"

"The initial charge—it came from her laptop. Trina was the target all along."

CHAPTER TEN

(♆)

WALT WAS NOWHERE to be found. Sean and Trina searched the historian's floor, the cafeteria; then she led her bodyguard to Building One, where Erica's office was located. The oldest building in the Yard, Building One had been Rear Admiral Dahlgren's home and office during the Civil War. President Lincoln was said to have visited Dahlgren often during the war, and a portrait of the president hung in the entryway. Trina couldn't enter the building without feeling a shiver of pride, and nodded to the Great Emancipator on her way up the stairs to Erica's office—which had once been Dahlgren's.

Whenever she visited Building One, she suffered serious office envy. The underwater archaeologists didn't suffer the whack-a-mole-like housing of cubicle life. Erica's office was large, with a view of the Anacostia River and plenty of sunlight. But she did have to share the space, and today her officemate, Undine, was at her desk. Undine had been out of town for most of the summer overseeing the underwater excavation of a Navy airplane in Lake Superior, and Trina forgot she was due back this week. Unfortunately, she didn't have time for a lot of chitchat. "Hey, Undine, I'm looking for Walt. Have you seen him today?"

"Trina!" Undine jumped to her feet and gave Trina a bear hug, which she returned. "How are you? I just heard—"

"I'm fine. And I can't wait to go out for beers and hear about your summer, but I *really* need to find Walt. Any clue where he is?"

"God, no. He avoids the underwater group as if he's afraid estrogen contact will make him start menstruating."

Behind Trina, Sean laughed.

Undine's smile lit up her face, and she held out her hand. "Undine Gray. And if you aren't *with* Trina, newly single."

Sean laughed again, shook her hand, and introduced himself as Trina rolled her eyes. Undine was back, and frankly, she'd missed her. Undine was unabashedly forward—the best drinking buddy a single girl in a big city could ask for.

"Sean is not *with* me, and I can't wait for you to explain the word 'newly,' but we don't have time now. Lunch tomorrow?"

"Sure. Sean, you available for dinner tonight?"

"Busy. Sorry."

Undine flashed her Julia Roberts-like wide smile. "Trina can give you my number."

Again Trina rolled her eyes as she led Sean back down the stairs. Outside and out of earshot, Sean said, "Who was that?"

"The biggest flirt at NHHC."

"Sounds like she's on the rebound." Sean opened the door and held it for Trina.

She stepped inside. "She's on permanent rebound. Hung up on a guy since forever. I love her to death, so that's the only warning I'll give you."

"Fair enough." Turning serious, Sean said, "I think Walt took off."

"Yeah. Bastard. Let's find Cressida and Mara. Maybe they know where he went." Trina led Sean to the basement conservation lab, Cressida's lair, as she catalogued the contents of the mystery file cabinet, which, fortunately, hadn't been filled with VD cleansing syringes.

Cressida glanced up from the camera table, where an old map was laid out under bright lights. Mounted on a frame above the map was a wide-angle digital camera that took high-resolution photos of documents. She straightened a bit at seeing Sean, and Trina wanted to laugh. Her bodyguard certainly had an effect on women.

Cressida caught her smile. "What? I have a boyfriend, but that doesn't mean I'm blind."

For his part, Sean just smiled and crossed his arms, showing off his thick biceps in his black T-shirt. He was as ripped as Keith and possibly even as good-looking. And he knew it.

"Cress, I'm looking for Walt or Mara. Have you seen either one?"

"I haven't seen Walt at all today. Mara was here, but she got a call from Curt about ten minutes ago and bolted. I think she's looking for you."

Sean's cell phone rang. He answered and, after a pause, said, "We're in the basement conservation lab with Cressida."

A minute later, rapid footsteps sounded on the stairs, and Keith appeared. He headed straight for Trina, wearing an intense, charged expression that caused her belly to flip. He pulled her to his chest and his thick arms circled her. Lips touched her forehead, then found her mouth for a hard, fierce, but sadly brief kiss.

Still holding her, he said, "Damn, I was worried about you. We've got to get you out of here."

His tone caused another belly roll, but this time not in a good way. "What's going on?"

"I assumed Mara already told you."

Now she was scared—and confused. "I haven't seen her. I think we've been circling each other as we searched for Walt."

"They were able to piece together fragments of the bomb." He paused. "It was in your computer."

The blood drained from Trina's face, possibly even her heart. She might have fallen if it weren't for Keith's encircling arms. After a moment, she stepped backward out of his embrace, grabbed a chair, and dropped into it. "My computer?" She had to force the words out, which was difficult because she couldn't breathe.

Keith nodded. "We left it by the front door, just inside, leaning against a structural wall. The gas furnace was only six feet away on the other side of that wall, in the garage."

She grappled with the news. "What set it off? Was it on a timer?"

"They haven't been able to identify enough pieces to be certain, but odds are it was tied to the computer clock. My guess is, your trip to see me was unexpected. No one could have guessed you would head to my house—which is why you had to be the intended target."

She considered that day. "They couldn't have known I'd take the computer out of the office. I left work a little early, but the Metro took forever—the trains were packed when I changed to the Orange Line at L'Enfant. By the time I got to your place, it was after five. Government offices clear out at five almost without fail. Why rig my computer to blow after working hours? Why rig my computer to blow at all?"

Keith knelt before her and gripped her hands. "Do you usually take your computer home?"

"Once a week—if that. I only had it that day so I could work on the Metro, since I'd left the office early."

"So if you hadn't brought the computer with you, it would have exploded on your desk."

She nodded, grasping at the one thing that comforted. "Most—if not all—of the historians on my floor would have left the office already."

Keith released her hands and turned to the staircase. "I want to check out your cubicle, then I'm getting you out of here."

They found Mara in Trina's cubicle, flipping through the mess of papers on her desk. She glanced up and said, "You heard?"

Trina nodded. "My guess is someone wanted to destroy the office." She glanced around the floor—taking in the central location of her cubicle. The proximity to Walt's.

"I was thinking the same thing," Mara said. "But why? The only thing of interest in here was the top-secret cabinet. And it's been moved—and declassified." She turned to Cressida, who had followed them along with Sean. "Have you found anything in the cabinet that warrants blowing up the office?"

"Hell, no. It's mostly maps. Really old, really out-of-date maps."

Mara pushed aside the stack of papers she'd been rifling through. "Bomb specialists are coming to search your cubicle, see if there's any explosive residue or fingerprints. They're headed to your apartment too."

"I doubt they had access to the building," Sean said, "or the bomb would have been planted in something stationary."

"Prior to Monday, when was the last time your computer left the office?" Keith asked.

Trina thought back, but this question wasn't hard. "I had it home that whole weekend—so I could e-mail you from my official work account."

Keith nodded. "You and Cressida were out for hours on Sunday when you went to the party. The computer was in your apartment then?"

"Yes."

Keith pulled out his cell and punched some buttons. "Dominick, the computer was at Trina's the weekend before." He met Trina's gaze. "Where in your apartment was it?"

"Either the kitchen table or in a laptop bag on the floor by the bookshelf."

"Did you ever notice it was moved? Or anything else strange?" Keith asked.

She closed her eyes and thought about the weekend. Nothing unusual before the party. And after—she'd been too angry with Keith to pay attention. "I don't know." It didn't help that she was somewhat prone to clutter.

To Curt, Keith said, "I'm taking Trina to the safe house, then heading to Walt Fryer's home. I have a few questions for him."

"I'm going with you," Trina said before he could hang up.

"It's not safe for you." Keith's tone was firm.

She bristled. "I'm the one who needs to ask him about the bullshit interview with Lieutenant Ruby."

Keith listened to his phone, then said, "Fine," and hung up. "I'm taking you to the Department of Justice—investigators need to interview you again anyway. Curt will send an agent to Walt's house. If he's there, they'll bring him to the DOJ, and you can be there while he's questioned. Mara, Curt wants you there too. Since Walt works for you, the situation could become complicated."

This was all so incomprehensible, Trina felt like she was spinning. "You and Curt both really think Walt and Lieutenant Ruby have something to do with the laptop explosive?"

Keith shrugged. "It's the only lead we've gotten so far."

They agreed Sean would drive Mara to Curt's office later, after she spoke with the investigators who would search Trina's cubicle. Keith insisted on taking Trina to the DOJ immediately.

Once they were alone in Keith's car—a Raptor vehicle on loan from Alec—the emotions she'd been trying to hold in check since her initial reaction in the basement rose to the surface. He reached for the gearshift, but she put out a hand and stopped him. "It's my fault your home blew up. Tyler's home was destroyed..." Her voice trailed off as the enormity of it hit her.

"Babe—"

Her body started to shake. "I'm sorry. So sorry. You lost...everything. Your library..."

"It's all just stuff." He squeezed her fingers. "It's not your fault. You didn't know—and we still don't know why."

"Your library was beautiful. Organized. I bet you even had a database, listing all the books."

He stroked her cheek. "Have. My computer was backed up.

Cloud."

Somehow that made her even sadder. "So you have a list of all the books you no longer own."

One corner of his mouth kicked up, and he rubbed his thumb across her bottom lip. "And a new quest to replace every one."

Something in her heart melted in that moment. Admittedly, she didn't have far to go—she'd been half in love with him after their night together. This just tipped her to the other side.

She pulled his face to hers and kissed him as she'd wanted to from the moment he'd appeared in the conservation lab. Her tongue met his in a hot, deep kiss that made promises she was more than eager to keep.

He groaned. His large palm cupped the back of her head, holding her to him as he deepened the kiss. With a pant, he released her. "Much as I want to, this isn't the time or place to finish that. Someone planted a bomb in your computer, and we're exposed out here."

"I suppose. But I've been fine all week."

"And you've had a bodyguard all week, and you've been working on a secure military base. Anyone desperate enough—and technically skilled enough—to break into your apartment and rig a bomb inside your laptop without you discovering it, is going to try again. We can't give him—or her—the opportunity."

"You're going to lock me up in a safe house and leave me there, aren't you?"

"No, my plan is to take you to the house where I've been staying, but whether or not that's a good idea will depend on what we learn from Walt."

(Ψ)

CURT DOMINICK HAD a reputation for being driven, ruthless in the courtroom, and cold in general. Rav had also told Keith that the man had studied karate with the same dedication he'd studied law, and after thirty years was a seventh-degree black belt who kicked Rav's ass during sparring about half the time. Given that Rav was a former Army Ranger who owned a private security company and military training ground that required him to remain in fighting shape, that was saying something.

Dominick hugged Trina and pressed a kiss to her cheek, then he shook hands with Keith, and sized him up. "Mara made me promise I wouldn't go Neanderthal and throw a fit about her playing decoy for you."

Trina flashed a sheepish grin. "Tell Mara I said thanks."

Dominick offered her a hint of a smile. "I don't know why I believed she wanted to go clothes shopping. Usually I can read her better than that."

She chuckled. "Yeah, I felt foolish for missing that clue too."

He circled back to his desk and dropped into a stately leather chair. Trina sat in a guest chair opposite. Keith was too wound up to sit, and stood just behind and to the side of her, a sentry, ready to protect and defend.

"Right before you arrived, I received an update," Dominick said. "Walt Fryer is in the hospital."

Trina gasped. "Why—?"

"Myocardial infarction. He collapsed on the Metro on the way to work today. He never made it into the office."

"How is he?" she asked.

"His prognosis is good. Apparently, this wasn't his first heart attack."

She sighed. "Suddenly, the idea of reaming him out for blindsiding me with Lieutenant Ruby makes me feel guilty."

Dominick lifted a stack of papers from his desk. "Mara found Ruby's file in Walt's cubicle and faxed his service record to me. It appears Ruby was caught up in the Tailhook scandal in 1991."

Keith bristled. "Walt sent a woman to interview an aviator who had a history of sexual harassment and misconduct?"

"So it appears. After he was discharged, he claimed it was because he was a whistleblower, and he was fired in retaliation. He produced some documents related to a botched flight mission that had been classified. He faced charges for revealing government secrets and spent most of the nineties embroiled in legal disputes with the US government. By all accounts, he's devolved into an antigovernment conspiracy theorist."

Unease trickled down Keith's spine. Could Ruby have moved in the same circles as his father? Keith had told Dominick everything—the background check would reveal his dad's activism easily enough, so he'd been upfront—and given their estrangement, it shouldn't be an issue. If Keith discovered any link between his father and Ruby, he'd do a hell of a lot more than block his e-mail address once and for all.

Dominick fixed Trina with a neutral gaze. "I'd like to hear the recording of your meeting with Ruby."

She pulled out a digital recorder from her purse and hit Play. Keith clenched his hands into tight fists as he listened. It was probably good that Sean had been on guard duty. Keith might have crippled Ruby. As it was, he gave Sean props for his quick reaction.

Recording complete, Curt plugged the USB end of the recorder into his computer and copied it. "I'm going to send this to the Secret Service and FBI for voice analysis. We have recordings of anonymous threats to the president and government made over the years. It would be nice if we could make a match. The man you met was definitely Lieutenant Brian Ruby? You saw his photo in the service file?"

"Yes. His service photos are twenty years old, but I believe he was the same man." She leaned back in her chair. "I don't get it. Why would Walt, a Navy employee, be interviewing an antigovernment activist?"

"According to Walt's files, Ruby contacted him with the claim he had info on the Navy's involvement with UN peacekeeping missions. Walt seemed to think it related to his short-term assignment after Desert Storm."

Keith leaned on Curt's desk. "So this wasn't a report assigned to Walt by the department?"

Curt met his gaze. "As far as we can tell. Mara knew nothing about it. Damn strange, and we can't question Walt right now. Probably not for a few days."

Shit. They only had more questions and no answers. "Is there any chance the heart attack was triggered?" Keith asked. "Could it be part of whatever is going on?"

Curt nodded. "It's possible. I've requested blood tests to determine if there are any chemicals in his system that could mimic or trigger a heart attack, but it will be days before we know anything."

Keith rubbed his hand across his face. "I'm taking Trina to the safe house, then I'm going to Ruby's."

"You can't question him, Hatcher. He's officially the subject of an FBI investigation."

Keith wasn't an FBI agent and no longer served in the US armed forces, so he didn't see how that mattered to him at all.

CHAPTER ELEVEN

THEY WERE BARELY inside the door of Keith's safe house before he had Trina pinned to a wall with his mouth on hers as he boosted her up so she could wrap her legs around his hips. She groaned and pressed her center against him, loving the feel of his thick erection even though her slacks and his jeans separated them.

His lips moved to her throat, sending erotic chills up and down her spine. "Babe." His lips moved lower. "I've wanted you ever since you left the hotel room this morning." He ground into her and kissed her again, then pulled back. "Unfortunately, Sean's going to be here in about two minutes."

She bit his bottom lip. "Plenty of time for you."

He let out a bark of laughter and gently slapped her bottom. "I'll make you pay for that later." He kissed her one more time, then loosened his grip. She unhooked her legs from his waist and slid down his body until her feet touched the ground.

"Promises, promises."

She left the foyer, eager to explore the house where she'd be staying with Keith for the foreseeable future. Small, clean, modern. Just outside the Beltway in Maryland, it was far from work, but she still wasn't certain if she'd be going to the office or working from here.

Damn if this wasn't the strangest ten days of her life. Freaky, scary lows, but also, Keith. Just being near him sent her endorphins flying. Looking at him made her knees weak, but it was the quiet moments and conversation that had her falling in love with him.

She circled the living room, looking for clues to him, but he'd lost everything in the explosion. This house wasn't his, nor was the furniture. Her gaze landed on a book on the end table, and her breath caught. Not just any book. *Her* book. Adapted from her dissertation on the Navy's role in the Cold War, the book represented four years of her life and was her proudest accomplishment.

And the guy who'd found her G-spot last night—and made good use of the knowledge—was reading it.

Damn if she didn't feel a tingle there again.

He stepped up behind her and slipped his arms around her waist. "I've read a lot of history books, and I mean it when I say you have a great voice for narrative history. I love the fact that it's a politically charged war, yet I'm halfway through and I have no clue what your politics are."

She smiled. His praise might just mean more to her than that of the small academic press editor who'd initially accepted the book for publication. She turned to face him, and his hands settled on her hips. "History is always written by the victor, giving most historical accounts biases. I believe the historian's politics have no place in narrative history. We shouldn't research the past only to support preexisting beliefs. We should present both sides and let the reader form their own opinion."

"I hope you intend to write more along these lines in the future."

"Maybe someday. I was actually thinking—" She stopped, then decided she may as well tell the truth. No secrets. "If I'd been able to convince you to tell me about Somalia, combined with my research into the Navy's other interventions to halt the rise of al Qaeda in East Africa, that it might be a good topic for another book. In the declassified parts, anyway."

He frowned, but his hands didn't leave her body.

"I know you aren't going to tell me. And I'm not with you because I'm holding out hope you will."

His expression cleared. "Good." He traced her jawline, then her cheek. The way he touched her made her feel beautiful, alluring. Like she was precious. "I want this to work between us, Trina. I—" He stopped.

Her heart raced, and she didn't think she could form words if she tried, so she waited.

"I've never—" He laughed and tucked his face in her neck, breathed deeply, then met her gaze again. "I've never felt like this with anyone before."

Trina didn't know which stunned her more: that this big, alpha, perfect former SEAL was nervous, or that he was nervous while saying he had deeper feelings for *her*.

She cleared her throat. "I'm falling for you too, Keith."

His smile lit up his face. The chiseled cheekbones went from handsome to stunning. His thick, dark brows lowered as his eyes flashed with heat. "Glad to know we're on the same page."

Heat infused her. This moment felt almost too good to be true. "Ironic that we have Walt to thank for meeting."

Those handsome brows drew together. "Even if he is somehow behind the explosion, I'm pretty sure we'd be following this same path without it. I distinctly remember carrying you up to my bedroom *before* the blast."

"Yes, but it was Walt who passed the Somalia assignment to me. He hates anything more recent than World War II, and once I passed the latest security clearance bringing me up to his level, he was more than eager to dump his assignments on me."

"When?" he asked, new urgency in his voice.

She thought back. "I tried to get ahold of you for at least two weeks. I had your Norfolk address at first. It wasn't until the week before we met that I found the Falls Church address. I probably had Walt's files for a few days before I started contacting sources, including you."

"What other projects did he pass on to you?"

"A Cold War one"—she glanced at her book on the table— "which happens to be my specialty, so it made sense, and the Panama invasion—Operation Just Cause, SEAL Team 4. Most of those interviews are done. Just some follow-up needed."

Keith studied her with a frown. "And you didn't have a problem with Walt dumping his work on you?"

She'd put up with so much crap from Walt already; she hadn't given it much thought at the time. "I'm low woman on the totem pole. Most of my coworkers have been there for decades. Everyone dumps their projects on me." She realized Keith's expression indicated he was angry for her sake, not that he was disappointed she hadn't stood up for herself in the office. Warmth flared low in her belly. "It's not a problem, because generally, I *love* my job. I'm a military historian working for the Navy. Do you have any idea how hard it is for an historian to get a steady job outside of academia? My mom was worried I'd end up teaching high school. Don't get me wrong—I had the best history teachers in high school, which is why I love the subject—but teaching…not in my skill set. And dealing with high school students? Shoot me now. My teachers—it was their calling. This is mine."

She'd pushed away from him and paced the room as she talked. She stopped and remembered her point. "So, no, in general, it doesn't bug me when Walt dumps his work on me. I was irked when he gave me the Ruby interview, because he told me about it at Dr. Hill's party like it was a done deal. But that was different. Mara makes sure he's loaded up with his precious World War II projects, so it isn't like he's napping while I do all the work. A few times, when a project timeline was too tight for me, she'd reassign it or kick it back to Walt."

Keith's body radiated with tension, as if he were connecting dots she hadn't realized existed. "How often is an historian assigned to analyze an event that occurred only five years ago?"

She cocked her head. His words were an acknowledgment that something *had* happened in Somalia five years ago, but then, he'd slipped along those lines before. "Very, very rarely. This was my first time. But it makes sense. Knowledge is power, and this study could help troops more now than if we waited fifteen years, at which point the players would have changed and the dynamics of East Africa will have shifted."

"And since I won't tell you anything, what are you going to do?"

She shrugged. "The report isn't dependent on your cooperation. I have other sources I intend to pursue."

"You're still going to write it." His tone was clipped, possibly angry.

She met his gaze and wasn't certain she liked the guarded look in his eyes. "Of course."

He stepped back, distancing himself from her. *Definitely angry.*

"Keith, if there's something you want to tell me, you *can* set the record straight. Think about how much your account could help SEAL teams on future covert ops."

His lips flattened. "No."

Whereas a minute ago she'd felt fluttery and doe-eyed, now tension had entered the room and stood between them, as tangible as another person.

A knock on the door sounded, breaking the silence but leaving the tension intact. Sean had arrived.

Chapter Twelve

WITH TRINA ENSCONCED in the safe house and guarded by Sean, Keith had chosen to burn his antsy energy by taking over the Ruby surveillance detail. It was only two in the afternoon, yet a week's worth of events had happened since he'd woken up in bed with Trina this morning.

He'd settled in an upstairs bedroom of an abandoned, boarded-up house a block away from Ruby's apartment. The house was one of many in the run-down neighborhood; clearly Ruby had fallen on hard times after his stint as a vaunted naval aviator. Keith trained his high-powered scope on Ruby's front window and brought him into crisp focus.

But Keith was distracted. His mind raced as he considered what other sources Trina might tap for information on the Somalia op. No one on his team would talk. Except Owen.

And Owen was no longer in rehab.

Shit. A conversation with Trina wouldn't be good for Owen or for Keith. Probably not for Trina either.

Hell, it would be bad for Josh and everyone on his team.

For the first time, it crossed his mind to tell her. She'd understand the implications. But this went far deeper than typical relationship trust—and they'd only known each other for a short time. No way. Kicking that hornet's nest could serve no purpose. She didn't need to know. She *couldn't* know. This wasn't something that could be filed away and forgotten, like the old cabinet Trina had told him about.

He'd been promised by the powers-that-be the op would never be declassified—there wasn't even any sort of written record at all—because if someone opened up this baby sixty years from now, there were likely to *still* be repercussions.

The Pentagon knew what happened, and they'd covered it up nicely. Why the op had been tossed to NHHC for analysis in the first place made no sense—and he had a feeling that was where they needed to be looking. He suspected someone wanted a new narrative—and they were sidestepping the official channels to get it. Hoping for an inaccurate—and public—report that couldn't be corrected because the truth had to remain buried for every country involved. Problem was, there was only one person who could play scapegoat if any portion of the truth came out.

Keith could well find himself wearing goat horns—and the woman who would crown him was the same woman he was falling in love with.

♆

TRINA HUNG UP the phone. She hadn't expected to get through to the former SEAL so quickly. She'd run into a dead end when she tried to track him down two weeks ago. But today, when frustration with Keith's attitude pushed her to try one more time, he'd answered the phone at his aunt's home.

Even more shocking, the man was eager to speak with her, and he was in the DC area. Now to convince Sean to take her to the interview.

Sean crossed his not insignificant arms and leaned against the wall. "Not gonna happen."

"If we meet at the Navy Yard, it'll be secure. You can sit in on the entire interview."

"No. I can't. I don't have your security clearance. You know it. He knows it. I sit with you, and your interview goes nowhere. So it's not. Going. To happen."

"Then we'll meet in the conference room in Building One. You can be right outside the door."

"Keith would kick my ass if I took you there."

Well, Keith wasn't here, was he? No, he'd left minutes after Sean arrived, without bothering to explain where he was going. He'd just kissed her—admittedly, it had been a spectacular kiss—but still, he'd left, leaving all the tension between them with her, where it filled her gut and wreaked havoc in her mind. "I am not an object Keith owns, nor am I a prisoner without freedom. If you won't take me, I'll call a cab."

"Don't be stupid."

"I'm trying *not* to be stupid. I'm trying to get my bodyguard to take me to my office so I can complete an assignment issued by the Pentagon." She glanced at her watch. This had been one long-ass day, and it was only two fifteen. She'd woken up in bed with Keith, which had been perfect, the best morning after. *Ever.* But the day had seriously gone to hell from there, culminating in Keith making it clear he was withholding information. And with everything that had happened, she'd begun to wonder if he was withholding evidence.

She might be falling in love with him, but she was still pissed. He could just *tell* her what she needed to know, but he'd refused, repeatedly. He didn't seem to get the fact that a report on Somalia could do some good—maybe even save the lives of other SEALs. So she did what any self-respecting historian would do—she found a former SEAL from his unit who was ready to talk.

"I'm calling Keith and telling him where I'm taking you."

"Call him. But he's not my keeper." Trina grabbed her purse—the only thing she had, because she hadn't returned to her apartment before coming here—and headed for the door.

She waited in the passenger seat of Sean's sedan. He joined her a minute later. "Keith's pissed."

"Tell him that makes two of us."

"I will not do that."

She snorted. "Today isn't going as you expected, is it?"

He tapped on the steering wheel. "Hardly."

"Yeah. Same here." She settled back in her seat and tried to ignore the heartache that increased with every breath.

"I don't like Building One for the meet place—and Keith doesn't either. We're going back to the DOJ."

"Fine," she said. "I'll call Curt and Lieutenant Bishop to make arrangements while you drive."

Thirty minutes later, they passed through the security screen and entered the Justice Department, where they were led to a private conference room. Sean stepped outside when Lieutenant Owen Bishop arrived.

Bishop was about the same age as Keith, but tall and skinny with hollow eyes. Clearly combat hadn't been good for him. He suffered a world of nervous tics. It was a hot summer day, stifling in the paved city, but Bishop wore a long-sleeved shirt, buttoned at the wrists.

Between his choice in clothing, the twitches, and his anxious start-and-stop speech pattern, it wasn't a huge stretch of logic to guess Bishop was self-medicating—most likely with heroin—but she suspected other substances were in the mix. He wasn't the first veteran she'd interviewed who'd turned to drugs to fight PTSD, and her heart broke for him even while wondering if his account of the Somalia op would be reliable.

But she'd taken this risk and very possibly screwed up her developing relationship with Keith in pursuing this interview, so she might as well see it through. Dammit, she hated it that Sean was right about her behaving stupidly. She should have known no fit SEAL would agree to an interview.

Sorrow for the man who fidgeted at the table filled her. His service to his country had resulted in trauma that led to pain and mental breakdown, which he'd failed to remedy with drugs. And now the man, who was once the best of the best, was a shell that symbolized the lowest of the low.

A junkie, full of self-loathing, with compromised mental acuity.

She set her digital recorder in the center of the table and pressed the Record button. "Why don't we start with the day your team arrived in Mogadishu?"

CHAPTER THIRTEEN

SONOFABITCH.

Keith should have covered Owen's aunt's house like Josh asked him to do. Once again, he'd let Owen down, Josh down. Hell, he'd let his whole team down. Keith's gut reaction was to leave and sit in on Trina's interview with Owen. No way would he talk if Keith were sitting right there. His relationship with Trina would be over—no way would she forgive him for sabotaging her interview—but dammit, it was over when she arranged to interview Owen. He doubted he'd be able to forgive *her*.

She's just doing her job.

No. It would never be that simple. Because what had happened in Somalia was anything but simple, and whoever had set Trina to researching it had to have an agenda. Unfortunately, as far as he knew, the person who had approved the assignment was the attorney general's wife. And at the time of the Somalia op, her uncle had been the vice president of the United States.

Andrew Stevens had certainly known what happened that day. The question was, did Mara Garrett? Had she given Trina this assignment, knowing full well the ramifications?

He couldn't imagine why she would do that, but he didn't know Mara, and he didn't know Curt. Rav's friends or not, they could have an agenda.

Pressure built in his head. Curt Dominick was personally overseeing this entire investigation. For all intents and purposes, he *was* the Justice Department. Keith had no way to sidestep the attorney general.

He had to have faith Dominick was one of the good guys, but he wasn't quite there yet. Now Trina was headed to the DOJ, and there was nothing he could do about it. Sure, that meant the questioning wouldn't happen in Garrett's realm, but her husband's might not be any better. He should have suggested Rav's house. Except Rav was in the middle of a contentious campaign. The last thing he needed was a woman who had been a bomber's prime target and a drugged-out former SEAL on his doorstep.

Shit. Keith didn't know what to do about his spotter. It had taken him months to get Owen into rehab—half the guys from the team had pitched in to cover the enormous fees—and now he'd bailed after a little more than a month into the six-month program.

He loved the guy like a brother…and at times resented him like a brother too.

And that didn't even take into account the guilt of being the cause of Owen's condition.

Had Trina contacted Owen and convinced him to leave the program? That would be…reprehensible. Unforgivable. The woman he was involved with couldn't want her history book that badly. Unless he'd misread her completely.

How well did he really know her? Shit, now he was questioning everything, delving into the places where he was most vulnerable.

Movement inside Ruby's home made him shake his head. Dammit. He wasn't focused.

Ruby answered a phone call, then stood in the window with the phone to his ear. Keith wished Alec didn't have rules against Raptor hacking cell phones and listening in, but that was the type of thing the former CEO had done, and it was sort of illegal…and unethical. But this guy knew something, and Keith considered ethics overrated when it came to the bastards who had tried to kill Trina, not to mention blowing up his house.

The man left the window. Minutes ticked by. More than anything, he wanted to go to the DOJ and haul Owen out of there before Trina could delve into the heart of his reason for self-medicating. But Keith had stupidly sent the guy on surveillance home, and now there was no one else to watch the front of the house. Another Raptor operative had the rear fire escape and windows covered. There were no other exits. This was a two-man job, and it would take at least an hour for Keith's replacement to get here if he wanted to leave and intercept Owen.

Why had Ruby, an antigovernment activist, requested an interview with Walt in the first place?

What if…

No.

His father didn't even know Keith had been in Somalia.

Trina knew, but she had access to his service record, while his father didn't.

He thought back to his visit with his dad three months ago. A last-ditch effort to salvage a relationship, it had been a fiasco. The only saving grace was seeing his brothers briefly at the end.

While he was there, Josh had called him several times. They'd been trying to work out the arrangement with the rehab center for Owen. Had he uttered the word "Somalia" at a time when his dad could overhear? They'd certainly discussed Owen's injuries from five years ago—the rehab center needed his full medical history. His dad knew Owen was his spotter. If he'd picked up that Owen was injured five years ago and had an inkling they'd been in Somalia, it could have set his bastard father on a quest to connect the dots. And his dad was brilliant at connecting—even when there were no dots.

He picked up his cell, then hesitated. But there was no one else to call. The attorney general answered immediately. "Dominick, there's a chance this could be about me after all."

"How so?"

"You need to dig to see if there's a connection between Ruby and my old man. Like I told you before, he's antigovernment. My dad might be trying to ferret out information on a classified SEAL op."

"Can you tell me any of your dad's avatar names?"

"No. I never read the crap he sends me."

Ruby's head appeared in the window again.

"Is there any chance your father is connected with WikiLeaks or RATinformant?"

Dread settled in his gut as he admitted the truth. "It's possible."

"We're working on a theory right now that Brian Ruby is one of the rats at RATinformant dot com."

Keith rubbed his forehead. Was it possible his dad was so far gone he'd joined up with government leakers to reveal top-secret information about military operations? Was his own father trying to destroy him? "I need to talk to Ruby."

"We have enough now to bring him in for questioning. I was just sending a team to his apartment."

"I want to be—"

Keith heard the pop first. The living room window he'd been

watching shattered. The backlit man dropped from view, but the spray of red on the wall beyond the window told Keith everything he needed to know.

Chapter Fourteen

TRINA REMAINED AT the table long after Owen Bishop left the conference room. She was surprised—and grateful—that Sean left her alone. She needed time to think. To gather herself. To figure out which way was up. And possibly the fastest route to get away from Keith.

No. Lieutenant Bishop hadn't—couldn't have—told the truth. If it were true, Keith would have been court-martialed. Imprisoned. Maybe even executed.

Except, a Pentagon cover-up would have been the first priority. There couldn't be a court-martial if there'd been no crime. And this crime sure as hell had not happened. At least, nothing had ever been leaked.

Trina had been in graduate school five years ago. Intensive study of current military action had been part of the coursework for a doctorate in military history. Today's news was tomorrow's history.

Somalia would forever trigger an association with the 1993 military action—the Battle of Mogadishu—that was described in the book and later movie titled *Black Hawk Down*. And for that reason, any military action in Somalia warranted notice. Nothing she'd read at the time hinted at what Bishop had described.

Cold sweat broke out on her brow. Jesus, she was just sitting still, and yet she was sweating. Shaking.

Keith was a sniper. He'd killed. She understood that. But this wasn't killing to serve his country. This was murder.

KEITH KNEW BETTER than to try to locate the sniper. Odds were the man—or woman—was long gone, and if not, Keith would only be making a target of himself. Dominick had told him to sit tight, he'd be there in a flash with federal agents.

Fortunately for Keith, he had an airtight alibi, having been on the phone with the attorney general when the shot was taken. Except…who was to say he hadn't taken the shot, then called Dominick? The Raptor operative couldn't help him. His view was limited to the back bedroom window. Ballistics would exonerate him, but that would take time.

He called Sean. "Is Trina still talking to Bishop?"

"No. He left five minutes ago."

Damn. "Put Trina on, then."

"She's still in the conference room."

Yet more dread snaked up his esophagus. "Alone—?"

"Yeah. Door's cracked open. I can see her. She's not in any danger. She's just…frozen. I'm guessing Bishop told her something she didn't want to hear."

Keith wanted to close his eyes. Or curse. Or smash something. But instead he said calmly, "I've got trouble here. Ruby is dead. Dominick and the feds are on their way. Keep Trina there. It's the safest place while we sort this out."

Sean swore. "Dead? How?"

"Sniper shot."

Sean let out a low whistle. "That's not going to look good for you."

Keith glanced at the sniper rifle on the floor next to him. He really should have left it in the trunk of his car, but some habits ingrained from years in the Navy were hard to let go. "No. It's not." He didn't make a denial, and Sean didn't ask for one. A point in the operative's favor.

"I'll keep Trina here, but she's going to ask questions."

"Tell her. She has the right to know about Ruby. About everything." *Except Somalia.* No. Only a select handful of people had the right to that information. But Keith had a feeling poor Owen had just broken the one and only vow that actually mattered.

He'd hung Keith out to dry. And the hell of it was, he couldn't go straight to Trina and separate fact from fiction from delusion.

$$\psi$$

TRINA PACED THE conference room. The tension in her gut had transcended to a point that could only be explained with particle physics. Operating on the usual three spatial dimensions plus time as the fourth, fear was now her own personal fifth dimension.

Fear that manifested as pain. Everything hurt more, lasted longer, intensified to the degree that even the blood rushing through her veins hurt.

Sean had purchased chocolate bars from a vending machine, but she couldn't face the sweetness of caramel or the salt of peanuts. All she could do was pace.

And wait. Finally, Keith stepped into the conference room and shut the door, leaving Sean and Curt on the other side.

"Did you do it?" Trina asked. A fear cramp nearly stopped her in her tracks.

"Do what?" Keith asked.

"Shoot him?" A surge of anger took over her tongue. "Wait, I suppose I need to be more specific with you—"

Keith flinched.

"Did you shoot Ruby?"

His eyes flashed with anger. "Hell, no. And I'm appalled you even asked."

But if Ruby knew, or was trying to uncover what happened in Somalia, Keith had motive. "My guess is I'm not the only one who's wondering." She nodded toward the door that blocked Curt from view. "I bet it was the first question Curt asked."

He took a step toward her, his broad shoulders stiff with tightly held fury. "It's *his* job to ask that question. Not yours."

She crossed her arms over her chest as if she could protect herself from the angry man—*murderer?*—who stood before her. At least Sean and Curt were right outside the door. One scream and they'd intervene. "I imagine my job is to fuck you and not ask questions like a good little girl. News for you, Keith. That's not me."

His gaze narrowed. "And that's not news."

"Did you shoot him because he knew the truth?" She almost had to choke out the question. The words felt raw on her tongue.

"I'm not a murderer." Keith's hands curled into tight fists.

"Really? Well, that will be news to your buddy Owen Bishop."

His head lowered, and he took a slow, deep breath. "Owen *is* my buddy, so I'll thank you to drop the sarcastic tone." He met her gaze again and continued, "And if I find out you had anything to do with extracting him from the rehab center I spent my last signing bonus getting him into, then we're done." He held his jaw so tight his lips barely moved.

"We're already done." She took two steps past him, toward the door.

Keith's hand on her arm stopped her. "Where is Owen?"

Her protective instincts flared. "Don't you *dare* hurt him."

His eyes flashed with a hard, harsh light. "I need to get him back to rehab. Tonight. He's just revealed details of an op he swore an oath to keep secret. He's bound to be looking to score heroin right now. I need to find him before he does."

Jesus. What have I done? "I reached him at his aunt's. He gave me a cell phone number. Lee Scott should be able to track him through the number." She retrieved the number from her phone, then turned again for the door.

Again, Keith's hand stopped her. The fingers that had touched her everywhere, that had made her gasp and cry out with pleasure, were now hard and unforgiving against the bare skin of her arm. "You aren't leaving without telling me what Owen told you. You owe me that much."

She paused. What did she owe him? She'd paid him back for the orgasms in kind. Dinner and a hotel room?

A few hours ago, she'd thought she owed him a town house, but now? She had a feeling this had been about him all along.

But fine, he wanted to know what Bishop said? She'd tell him. He was the only fucking person in the world she could tell, because there was no way this would ever go in any official Navy report, and he damn well knew it. "He said he was injured in a firefight that ensued after you fragged a UN force commander."

Keith's gaze dropped to the floor. For one brief moment, he had no poker face, confirming her accusation.

Pathetic, feeble hope that Bishop might have been wrong fled. "You did it, didn't you? You shot Major General Kassa."

He met her gaze straight on. "Yes." Then he marched to the door and jerked it open. "Dominick, take her to a new safe house. I'm done with her."

CHAPTER FIFTEEN

OWEN HAD REMEMBERED. He knew Keith had shot the East African major general who'd been in charge of his nation's UN peacekeeping force. It shouldn't surprise Keith, yet it did. When Owen was in recovery, he'd said he didn't remember anything for hours—maybe days—before he was injured. A blow to the head could do that to a man.

Keith and the team had agreed not to tell Owen—if he didn't remember, he couldn't tell anyone what had really happened. But obviously, at some point the memory had returned, and now it haunted him.

Based on Trina's hostility, Keith figured Owen hadn't remembered the context. He didn't understand *why*. His wound had required brain surgery. Physical therapy. He'd been in recovery for over a year.

Did he remember that Keith had made the kill shot without Owen, his spotter? If so, that would only confuse him more. And this wasn't just any kill shot, but one that had the potential to start an all-out war. Archduke Franz Ferdinand had nothing on a rising UN force commander—the number of countries involved...not to mention the treaties and the UN charter for the mission... A charter he'd violated with one bullet and a precision shot.

Keith hadn't wanted anyone on his SEAL team involved. But he'd needed help. Josh. Mikey. Leo. Owen. And Keith. The team he'd gathered to pull it off, plus five more who were in position in the camp should the op fall apart. In all, ten SEALs knew what went down, and Keith was confident no one but Owen would ever talk.

And for years, they'd clung to the belief Owen didn't remember.

In spite of everything, Keith would never, ever regret taking action. He couldn't have lived with himself if it had been another Srebrenica. But it seemed that without all the facts, Owen couldn't live with himself now. Add chronic pain from the head wound, and it was easy to see why he'd turned to drugs.

Lee was quick to agree to track Owen through his cell phone—no questions asked. Keith had a feeling Curt had vouched for him at some point, and he swallowed the bitterness of having gained Curt's and Lee's trust but not Trina's.

Well, that little experiment in attempting an actual relationship had burned out fast. His gut clenched as he followed Lee's directions, zeroing in on Owen's location based on pings from cell phone towers. What was he thinking getting involved with a woman who'd made it clear from the start that she wanted to expose Somalia?

And now… Would she?

She'd be fired. Top-secret clearance meant she could keep a secret, not expose it. And if she did… The only way the US could avoid retaliation would be if Keith paid the ultimate price. He'd have to admit he'd taken action without orders. Cop to treason, or worse.

Prison…. Hell, they could even send him to Gitmo. The NSA leaks, Snowden and the others, what they'd done was nothing compared to fragging a UN force commander. And Keith would never be able to reveal why. The Pentagon—his ally in the cover-up—would turn on him and nail his ass to the wall to avoid a complete breakdown of NATO and the UN.

Trina wouldn't do it. She couldn't. She was smart, if the letters PhD after her name meant anything. She'd understand the stakes. She'd keep her mouth shut. She wouldn't sell out her country for a book deal.

He hoped.

But then, this was the same woman who'd slept with him, then had the gall to ask him if he were a murderer. So maybe brains she had, but judgment of character? Not so much.

Face it, when it came to Trina, he'd been wrong from the start. He'd been thinking with his dick, and now he might end up paying the ultimate price.

What would it be like to be a SEAL locked up with a bunch of terrorists?

He'd take the fall for his country without question, but he'd swallow a bullet before he'd be consigned to Gitmo.

Another ping. This one a few blocks away. Deep in the run-down projects of southeast DC. Owen was definitely trying to score drugs. Keith had to find his spotter before the needle found a vein.

⟨Ψ⟩

CURT FACED TRINA across the conference table. Sean remained outside the room. "You need to tell me, Trina. I *do* have security clearance. Attorney general is a cabinet position."

Hell, as AG, the man was seventh in line for the presidency. But she couldn't form the words. Who the hell had put her up to this? And why? That was the question they needed to answer, and she'd told Curt that already. Mara had gone through her files and could find no record of the assignment. It had never passed through her, which meant it hadn't come from the Pentagon.

As far as they could tell, the assignment originated in Walt's e-mail, which made no sense.

Curt fixed her with a hard stare. "You said this directly relates to the bombing—at least you think it does—which means you are withholding evidence about what may have been a terrorist act. One that could have killed you. Keith. Your coworkers. Mara." His voice dropped on his wife's name.

This was so damn convoluted, she couldn't keep it straight. Mara's uncle had been vice president when Keith had shot the UN force commander. Andrew Stevens had to know what had happened. But she believed Mara when she said she knew nothing and had no part in the assignment falling to Trina. The woman was a patriot who'd devoted herself to bringing home the remains of servicemen and women prior to taking a job with the NHHC. No way would she be involved in trying to expose what had happened in Somalia.

"I can't tell anyone, Curt. Not even you. Some secrets are too big."

Shit. Wasn't Curt vetting Keith for the job with Raptor? Well, she'd nicely destroyed that dream for Keith. But then, Keith might be going to prison for murder. "Did Keith shoot Ruby?"

"No. He was on the phone with me when it happened."

"How do you know he didn't shoot him, then call you?"

"Because I had an FBI agent staking out the place too. I appreciate Raptor's assistance and wanted input from Keith, but make no mistake, this is an FBI investigation."

"I should have guessed that." Suddenly, she felt horribly dumb. Naïve. "You've been running the show the whole time, haven't you?"

"As much as I can. If we'd known you were the target from the start, you'd have been in protective custody. But since Keith was the likely target, I was content to let Raptor provide your security."

"You knew about Mara pretending to be me."

"Yes." He leaned back in his chair. "I'm not a controlling asshole. I wasn't having you—or Mara—followed. We were tracking Keith, but when my agents kept losing his trail, I contacted Alec Ravissant and insisted he keep me posted on Keith's whereabouts."

"Did Keith know this?"

Curt shrugged. "He signed a form authorizing a full background check. I wasn't required to provide details on my methodology."

"So he's been a suspect all along."

"No. Material witness. And if I didn't have the authorization, I'd have gotten a warrant. It was just easier since Keith signed off on the background check, and Alec had his own reason to keep me in the loop."

"But you don't trust Keith," she pressed. Her emotions toward him were so confused, she wanted Curt's take.

He leaned forward and studied her. Finally, he said, "There was a recommendation for a commendation for Keith in his file. I was curious about that. The reason stated seemed to be an unremarkable op in Afghanistan four years ago. It appeared, from the paper trail, the recommendation stalled in a very unusual place—the office of the vice president."

Trina sat up straight. "Mara's uncle?"

Curt nodded. "Last week, I went to visit Andrew."

The former vice president was currently in a minimum-security prison for white-collar criminals—and Curt Dominick was the man who'd put him there. "I don't imagine he was thrilled to see you."

"Quite the contrary, Andrew and I have become friends. Of a sort." He smiled. "Andrew wouldn't answer any of my questions when it came to Senior Chief Petty Officer Keith Hatcher. He only said the recommendation was ill-advised. Now, I don't know about you, but when a former vice president knows the name, rank, and service record of a random enlisted Navy SEAL—whom he has never met—I start to wonder."

Trina sat forward, uneasy with Curt's tone. "Whatever happened in Afghanistan must have warranted notice."

"But the Afghanistan op was insignificant, as I said. It's barely even classified. Andrew put the kibosh on a commendation, which makes me wonder if there is a dirty secret in Keith's past, something the top brass knows about—right up to the head of the executive branch." Curt's tone turned angry. "Something the Pentagon didn't condone but was forced to cover up. International relations get tricky when military action is involved."

She frowned. "But if he did something that awful, he'd have been forced from the Navy. Dishonorable discharge at the very least."

"Not if what he did was so bad the powers that be were forced to cover up his crime for him. Hell, if they tried to eject him he could threaten to expose the cover-up."

"At his own expense? That makes no sense. And if he did something that awful, surely he'd have a good reason? Keith is a good man. I've read his service record—it's exemplary. He's a patriot who enlisted right after September eleventh. He's given his entire adult life to the military. Surely he—" She stopped upon hearing the entreaty in her voice. And the ring of truth in her words.

Curt sat back and smiled. Then he winked at her.

Shit. She'd just been manipulated by a master. "You aren't suspicious of Keith at all, are you?"

"No. Everything I've learned about him in the last week tells me that whatever he did, he did it for a reason. You seemed to be the one who was struggling with doubt."

�

THE DRIVE TO the rehab center would take several hours, time Keith didn't have to spare. He'd called Josh, who agreed to take Owen back to rehab. The center had the right to refuse to let him back in—but if there was anyone who could convince them to take him back, it was Josh. He was a far better diplomat than Keith would ever be.

It made him ill to think of the jeopardy Josh, Owen, and the others faced. His fault. All his fault. He never should have reopened his door that Sunday morning after Trina said she wanted to know about Somalia. He should have deleted her e-mails unread. He never should have gotten involved with her.

He'd been selfish, reaching for what he wanted in spite of the risks. He had no right to endanger his team that way. And Trina was now in danger too.

Owen mumbled something. He was stretched out in the backseat. Not an OD, thank God. Just exhausted, stressed. He'd been tapering with meds in rehab and hadn't gotten his dose today. Withdrawal had kicked in. Owen was unable to sleep but also unable to think or argue. Thankfully, Keith had caught up with him before he'd scored.

Keith pulled up in front of Josh's small house in McLean, Virginia. Darkness had begun to fall, and the residential street was quiet. Josh met him out front, and they shook hands, then together they transferred a shaking, sweating Owen to the back of Josh's car, where he lay down across the length of the seat.

Keith met Owen's bleak, pained eyes before his head dropped onto the cushion, and he squeezed his eyes shut.

Keith placed a hand on Owen's ankle. "You'll beat this. We'll help you. Always."

"I told her. I told her everything." The words were muttered, hard to decipher, but the most coherent thing he'd uttered since Keith found him in the alley next to a liquor store trying to cut a deal. Owen grabbed his hair and pulled. "I'm sorry. I'm such a fuckup. I—" He choked on a sob. "I shouldn't have—" He twisted and buried his face in the seat.

"It's okay, Owen. We can trust her. She'll never tell. She'd never do anything to hurt you." *Or me.* The ache in Keith's gut began to ease. If he hadn't been so damn desperate to find Owen, he'd have seen that sooner.

He tucked Owen's legs up as if his friend were an invalid, closed the door, then leaned against it. "We need to know who lured him out," he said to Josh.

"I didn't get any leads at the rehab center and haven't been able to reach Owen's aunt. You've ruled out the historian?"

Remembering Trina's protective attitude toward Owen, he shook his head. "I don't think she knew he'd been in rehab. It's hard to believe she would have set up the meeting if she'd known."

He'd misjudged her, but then, she'd misjudged him too.

Josh nodded toward the back of his car. "Did you mean what you said to Owen? Can we trust her?"

"Yes. She's smart. She knows what's at stake." He rubbed a hand across his face. "However, from her attitude it appears Owen didn't tell her *why* I shot Kassa. My guess is he doesn't remember that part."

Josh frowned. "Whoever was so eager for her to find out about Kassa probably doesn't give a crap about why."

"Yeah. And that's a problem. I hate dropping Owen and running, but I need to get back to the city. She was set up. He was set up. Someone wanted her to know what happened, and that puts her at risk."

"You think their next move will be to go after her now that she has useful intel?"

Keith nodded. He believed manipulating Trina had been the goal from the start—because she was the best bet to get someone from Keith's team to talk—and now she knew something that had been deeply buried by no less than the Pentagon. A chill of fear slid down his spine. *She's well guarded.* He cleared his throat. "She's safe for the moment, but as soon as she leaves the DOJ, she's vulnerable."

Dammit, in the heat of anger, Keith had told Dominick to find her a new safe house. Dipshit move, which he'd correct the moment he got back on the road and could call the attorney general.

Josh frowned. "You shouldn't have left her."

"I needed to find Owen." And, truthfully, he'd needed to get his thoughts in order where she was concerned. "I left her with the AG. And a bodyguard. She's safe."

Josh opened the driver's door on his car. "Go find her. I'll call the others, bring them up to date, and take care of Owen. Stay safe."

Keith nodded. "You too."

Chapter Sixteen

CONSTITUTION AVENUE WAS busy as evening shifted to night, but then, Constitution was always busy. Sean was driving, and Trina sat in the passenger seat, feeling utterly defeated. They were headed to another safe house. One without Keith.

She might have inadvertently caused his friend to relapse and called him a murderer. He'd never forgive her, and she couldn't blame him.

Sean's cell phone rang, and he hit the Speaker button. "Bring Trina back," Curt said, his voice carrying more tension than he usually revealed. "I just heard from the team searching Ruby's apartment. We have confirmation the guy was a Julian Assange wannabe. Homeland Security has been looking for this guy ever since a website leaked sensitive Pentagon documents on an anti-US government website."

Cold dread spread from Trina's belly outward. "Are you talking about RATinformant dot com?"

"Yeah. It appears Ruby's avatar was Gopher. His partner Mouse is still at large."

Trina had never been to the website, but she knew thanks to the media coverage surrounding the Pentagon leak that the group capitalized the letters in RAT because they stood for "Revealing All Truths" and their avatars were all rodents: Gopher, Mouse, Muskrat, and Beaver, with Gopher and Mouse being the site owners and operators. Antigovernment activists with branding.

"Trina, we think they were trying to use you to get military secrets they could publish on the website. Mara's research into the initial assignment hasn't turned up a damn thing. All we know is it didn't come from the Pentagon or the Navy. She's trying to figure out how it got into Walt's e-mail."

Dread turned to nausea. She had met with Gopher, because he wanted to use her to get information he couldn't access otherwise. Before she took this job—and certainly before she'd completed the security clearance process—she'd been informed that any contact with WikiLeaks or RATinformant, or any of the other government leak websites put her at risk of being charged with communicating with the enemy. It was one of the reasons she'd never visited any of the freaking sites—even though some of the documents uploaded would probably help with her research.

Yet now it turned out she'd *met* with a RAT?

Her head throbbed. "I didn't know, Curt. And I didn't tell him anything."

"I know Trina. We've got your recording to back up your statement, and Sean was a witness. Come back to the DOJ. I've got a few more questions about—"

Curt's words were lost in the crunch and jolt as a car slammed into the rear quarter panel on Sean's side of the vehicle. Trina screamed as they careened to the side. Lights and direction were a blur.

Sean kept his head and shouted to Curt what was happening even as he righted the vehicle. Again, they lurched sideways as the vehicle pounded them again. But Sean had a firm grip and swerved to avoid the brunt of the impact.

She twisted in her seat to see the relentless vehicle—but all she saw was one blinding headlight as the car came at them again, this time from behind. Up ahead, cars were stopped at a red light. She braced herself as Sean slammed on the brakes. Struck from behind by the speeding car, they shot forward, rear-ending the car in front of them. Trina saw nothing but the white of the airbag.

ψ

KEITH WAS ONLY a block behind Trina and Sean and closing in when he saw the dark sedan slam into the side of their car. Stuck with a dozen cars between them, all he could do was watch in horror as the sedan struck the driver's side again, then finally rear-ended them when Sean was forced to brake.

Keith aimed for the curb and jerked to a stop, then sprang from his car and sprinted to the wreck, wishing he had his Glock at the small of his back, but DC gun laws prevented him from carrying concealed. He hesitated and considered grabbing his rifle from the trunk when the masked driver of the sedan jumped out of his car and circled to the passenger door—where Trina was likely to be seated. The man pointed a pistol at the front passenger window.

He had to be sweating under the ski mask on the hot summer night, and his wildly shaking arms said everything Keith needed to know. The guy was no operative. No military man.

Dominick had told him of Ruby's association with RATinformant when he'd called to get Trina's location moments ago. Odds were good this jumpy guy wielding a gun was Ruby's partner in exposing government secrets, the RAT known by the avatar Mouse.

Mouse was so focused on the car he'd just run down, he didn't even scan to check his six. He had no clue what he was doing. He slowly approached Trina's door at an angle. His back to Keith.

No time to grab the rifle, but Keith could take this amateur down without it. He darted to the side, so he could get a better view into the car. Trina appeared to be unconscious. He couldn't see Sean and wondered if he'd also been knocked unconscious, or if both were playing possum with Mouse.

It was clear Mouse didn't know what to do. Pointing a gun at an unconscious woman was futile. The man cursed and shouted instructions that garnered no response from Trina in her slumped-over position.

Keith charged, using a football tackle that slammed Mouse into the pavement. Keith stripped the gun and sent it skidding across the sidewalk. He pinned Mouse belly down with his hands behind his back, then torqued his gun arm, and the bastard howled with pain.

Keith leaned down and whispered in the prostrate man's ear, "You think you can go after the woman I love, and I won't kill you?" Rage had taken over as the image of Mouse pointing a gun at Trina eclipsed everything else.

Mouse sobbed and whimpered, unable even to thrash under the heavy weight of Keith sitting on his back. Slowly, the man's words broke through the angry haze. "The government killed Gopher. Now they're after me. Dr. Sorensen was my only hope for leverage. My only hope to stay alive."

From behind Keith, Sean said, "Thanks for the assist, Hatcher. I'll take over from here. The FBI will be here shortly."

Mouse screeched again. "No! They'll kill me. Like they did Gopher." He bucked upward, fear giving him strength.

Keith glanced behind him to see Trina—beautiful, perfect,

amazing Trina—standing slightly behind Sean. A scratch above her eyebrow dripped blood. The frame above the left lens of her glasses was cracked—probably damaged by the airbag. Keith lost his voice for a moment as he prayed that was her only injury.

Sean handed him a zip-tie, forcing Keith to focus. "Bind him."

Keith looped the plastic around Mouse's wrists, cinching it tight, while Sean did the same to the man's ankles. Then Keith lifted his weight from Mouse's back and flipped him over, then said, "Let's see who we have here."

Sean reached down and plucked off the ski mask, revealing a sweaty, freckled face that looked vaguely familiar to Keith. Then he remembered. He'd seen the guy at Rav's house, weeks ago.

Trina gasped. "Derrick Vole?"

CHAPTER SEVENTEEN

SIRENS SCREECHED AS an ambulance, a fire truck, and what seemed like a dozen police cars converged on the busy intersection. Sean yanked Derrick to his feet, and Trina made a beeline for Keith, unsure of the reception she'd receive but desperate to tell him her feelings.

Before she could get a word out, he caught her against him and kissed her, his tongue plundering her mouth with the same desperation she felt. She kissed him back but pulled away quickly and cupped his face. The police would need to interview them. They'd be separated, like they were after the bombing, and she needed to tell him. Now. "I'm sorry, Keith—I—"

"I know. I am too. I—"

She covered his mouth with her hand. She wanted him to hear her. "I think I'm falling in love with you, Keith. Maybe you think that's nuts because we barely know each other. But it's true. And I freaked out earlier, because I was scared. Scared to trust my instincts. Scared I was mistaking lust for something more. Scared I had no judgment when it came to you and that maybe I was horribly wrong. After what I did and what I said, you probably never want to see me again. I just wanted to tell you now, when I had the chance. Whatever happened in Somalia"—she glanced at Derrick, who remained a few feet away, and lowered her voice— "doesn't matter. I know the man you are. You had a good reason. I'm sorry I let my fear get in the way of seeing that. And I will never, ever ask for that reason. Some secrets must be kept."

His intense gaze didn't waver, even as medics and officers surrounded them. His eyes weren't angry, but neither were they forgiving. He'd probably only kissed her in the heat of adrenaline. She'd gone and brought emotion into the moment and he didn't want it. Didn't want her.

That was okay. She'd needed to say it. What he did with her words was up to him.

She slowly lifted her hand from his lips as the silence stretched between them. An officer approached and asked something, but she lacked the ability to focus on the words. The only person who mattered was Keith.

The light in Keith's eyes shifted. Warmed. One corner of his soft lips curled upward. Her heart, which had been racing, slowed and found a heavy bass beat. He leaned down. The breath of his whispery voice sent chills—the good kind—straight down her spine, and his words caused heat to blossom in all the right places. "After we're done with questioning, I'm taking you home and making love to you for hours. And then I'm going to spend the next week making sure you'll never again doubt the connection between us, never question the fact that I'm falling in love with you too." He kissed her again, softer but still deep. His tongue slid against hers in a warm caress that made her knees weak.

Tears burned against her eyes. This amazing man was hers. He could forgive her. She'd give anything to be alone so they could revel in this moment, but an insistent police officer wasn't in the mood to be ignored any longer.

"Sir, we have questions."

Keith released her with encouraging reluctance and faced the young uniformed officer. "We may as well wait for the FBI. This is going to fall under their jurisdiction."

The officer frowned and insisted on separating Keith and Trina so they could begin questioning, but as expected, minutes later FBI agents arrived, and the DC police were not very gently nudged from the investigation.

Questioning took hours. She was checked out by a paramedic early on, then again after Keith must have reported she'd appeared unconscious in the car.

She explained that she'd only pretended to be knocked out by the impact. Her favorite pair of glasses had cracked, but she could still wear them. She'd have a fair number of bruises and was sure to be sore tomorrow, but that pain hadn't settled in yet, and she felt fine. Exhausted but fine.

Derrick Vole had been whisked away, and many of the questions the FBI agents asked now centered on her association with him.

Vole. Well, of course, that must be where the rodent theme came from, his real last name. He must be the type who believed in his superiority to the degree that he planted his true identity in the name of his website and dared Homeland Security to find him.

What would Alec Ravissant do? Vole had been a key member of his campaign team. This would be a devastating blow, especially given the congressional investigation into Raptor's Alaska military training ground. A month ago, Alec had been a shoo-in to win the Maryland senate race, but when word got out that one of his campaign aides was Mouse, a government data leaker at RATinformant.com, poll numbers would plummet.

Finally, they were done with the preliminary questions, and Curt called and told Trina that he wanted Keith and her to be at the DOJ at noon the following day. They weren't going to question Vole until they'd finished searching both his and Ruby's apartments. Relieved to know she didn't need to sit through another grilling by Curt—at least not tonight—she found Keith conferring with Sean on the edge of the crowd of roadside investigators.

"You've been released?" Sean asked.

She nodded.

Keith patted him on the back. "I'll take over guarding Trina from here."

Sean chuckled. "Yeah. I figured. Rav said it's okay to cut me loose. We think she's out of danger now, but Rav wants you to take her back to the safe house tonight to be certain. Take a surveillance detection route to make sure the location remains secure. I'll watch the choke point."

Sean had explained those terms during his week of babysitting. All that mattered to her now was it meant it would take forever to reach the safe house, but Trina didn't care so long as she was with Keith.

She gave Sean a hug, then followed Keith down the road to his car, which had been moved during cleanup of the accident. Keith draped an arm around her shoulder, and she felt safe, comfortable, and like she was already home.

She was strangely wired on the long drive. It was after midnight, and the day had been brutal. By all rights, she should be passed out in the seat. But anticipation had a way of keeping her alert.

Keith parked in the safe-house garage, and the door rolled down behind them. They were alone. At last. She'd jump him in the car, except he'd already opened his door.

She began unbuttoning her blouse as she followed him to the interior door. Inside, she kicked off her shoes and dropped her blouse on the floor, then unzipped her slacks.

"Are you hungry?" Keith turned and startled at seeing her in only her bra and panties as she stepped out of her slacks. He slowly, deliciously, smiled.

"Yes. Very," she said and grabbed his shirt, pulling him toward her. Instead of kissing him, though, she pulled his shirt up, revealing his to-die-for abs, then his incredible pecs. He helped her by pulling the shirt over his head, exposing those wide shoulders and muscular biceps.

The guy had the most amazing body she'd ever seen, let alone touched. And he was all hers.

"I can see that," he said, his voice husky. She'd caught him off guard, but he was quick to catch up. She could tell because she felt his thickening erection as she worked his fly open. She slid her hand inside his pants and stroked the length. He let out a guttural groan that made her wet and ready.

They stood in a small hallway that connected the garage to the living room, and she nudged him toward the wall.

She *needed* to taste him. To hold him in her mouth. To feel his thickness on her tongue. To make him pulse with pleasure. She'd traveled a million emotional miles today, and this was where she wanted the journey to end, with her showing him how she felt with her hands, her mouth, her body.

Keith chuckled. "Uh-uh."

"No?" She took a step back. He couldn't be rejecting her. He was locked and loaded. This was *mutual*, dammit.

"No. Not here. Let's at least make it to the living room. And I want to go down on you first. I called dibs."

The sudden tension released as quickly as it had coiled. "You did not."

"I did. Silent dibs, in the car."

"Yeah, well, I called silent dibs when we kissed right after you tied up Vole."

"Yeah, well, I promised God when I dropped off Owen that if I found you tonight, I was going to tell you I'm crazy about you and make you come against my tongue at least four times. You can't make me break my promise to God."

"But your promise to God didn't define who gets to go down on whom first." She stroked his erection, determined to convince him she was right with whatever means necessary. "And did you really promise God that?"

"That's between me and God. And I think I just got harder with your use of the word 'whom' in a sexual context."

"Wait until you find out how else I can use my tongue in a sexual context."

Keith laughed and scooped her up. He carried her to the living room and set her on her feet. "First person naked gets to go down first."

Trina had a decent head start, but she'd miscalculated, because Keith only needed to kick off his shoes before removing jeans and briefs with one sweep, and she'd already opened his jeans for him, while she had to unhook her bra *and* slide down her underwear.

Keith won.

Which really wasn't such a tragedy when he positioned her on the couch and spread her thighs, then traced her opening with his finger, brushing over her clit with just the right amount of pressure to make every nerve in her body sing with heat and anticipation.

He leaned in and flicked his tongue across her clit, then slid a finger inside. She was slick and ready and fought the urge to demand he put his cock inside her immediately. She wanted to rush this, but Keith was showing no signs of being in a hurry.

Then he purred with pleasure. "God, you're beautiful. Sexy." He smiled. "And mine." On the final word, his tongue again stroked her clit, and the jolt of pleasure caused her to buck in response.

He continued to rub her with tongue and fingers, alternately sliding each inside her until she was in a frenzy, on the cusp and needing either his cock inside her or his tongue to push her over the edge.

But she was determined to turn the tables and rocked her hips back, breaking contact. "My turn." She tugged at his shoulders, encouraging him to stand before her. She took his cock into her hand and stroked the shaft, then slid to the floor to kneel before him and took him into her mouth.

His thick erection firm against her tongue, she sucked on the head then slid downward. She started slowly, inching down the shaft, then holding him deep before easing back with tight lips and stroking tongue, only to ease forward and take him deep all over again. She stroked his testicles as she sucked.

He groaned in response. "Trina. Babe. Oh God. You are— damn. Amazing. I can't—" The words came out in a slow tumble, arousing her as much as his mouth had moments before. She wanted to bring him to orgasm. To finish him with her lips and tongue. To feel his cock pulse in her mouth in a way she wouldn't feel if he were encased in a condom inside her.

From the sounds he made, he was right on the edge when he pulled back. "Babe—"

"Shut up and come." She took him deep again, sucking harder and faster, and his back arched as he came in hot bursts that made her feel sexy and powerful as she swallowed his ejaculate.

He dropped to his knees, bringing them chest to chest. "Babe. That was—" He kissed her neck and shoulder before dropping lower to take her hard nipple into his mouth. He rolled the tip with his tongue, then said, "Amazing." He grinned and kissed her. "I'm nuts about you, babe."

She kissed him back, loving the feel of his skin against hers, hot and ready after the pleasure of bringing him to orgasm with nothing but lips and tongue. His fingers found her opening and slid deep inside as his thumb stroked her clit.

She panted with the sudden pleasure. "I think you're pretty damn amazing too," she said against his lips as he quickly brought her to the edge of orgasm.

He pushed her backward so she lay on the floor. "My turn." His mouth trailed downward, across her skin, stopping at her breasts, then continuing onward, toward her belly button. Then lower still, until he reached the juncture of her thighs and again slid his tongue inside. He grazed her sensitive clit with his teeth, then sucked on it, causing her to thrash and suck in a deep panting breath.

He repeated the action, then stroked her with his tongue while sliding two fingers inside. She was so aroused—from his touch, from his smell, from the feel of his cock on her tongue—that it only took a moment for him to bring her to a hard, intense orgasm. She rocked from the repeated waves of pleasure as he applied pressure to her clit with his tongue, drawing out the orgasm from merely blockbuster to full epic.

Afterward, they lay entwined on the carpet, drenched in sweat as she caught her breath and came back to earth. "Wow."

His lips pressed to her shoulder. "Good word for it." He kissed her. "But we're not done tonight until you come when I'm buried deep inside you."

"Five minutes," she said. "That's all I need."

He chuckled. "Deal."

She idly traced his chest muscles as her breathing returned to normal. Contentment settled in, but with it, the barriers in her mind relaxed, and fears that she'd been squelching slipped past. She snuggled closer to Keith, as if being pressed against him could ward off the worries.

He turned toward her, and stroked her cheek. "You're thinking again, aren't you?"

She nodded. "Trying not to. Trying to just think about you and enjoy the moment."

"It's hard to compartmentalize. Hell, the Navy spent years trying to teach me, and I'm pretty good at it. But being here, with you. Now. Feeling this way—relaxed, crazy about you—it's harder to block the rest out. Plus, we have a lot going on."

"Vole," she said. "He works for your friend. For Alec. That's going to be bad for the campaign."

"Yeah." His mouth twisted in a wry grin. "Could seriously mess up the job offer—he's offered me the CEO position, if he wins the election."

Trina bolted upright. "Seriously? CEO? Isn't that like…a big deal?"

"Yeah. I'm scared as hell, but I have to take it. I mean, aside from the crap ton of money and health insurance, it's in a field I know. And it's not just what I know, it's what I'm good at. What I'm best at. I can train military personnel; teach them readiness that could save their lives. Plus…while I'll have to travel for work a fair amount, the headquarters are in DC—only a few blocks from the White House. And…you're here."

"If Alec loses, will there still be a job?"

"Yeah, but something smaller. Which would be fine. Frankly, I wouldn't mind starting on a lower floor."

"Curt is vetting you." She paused. "Somalia shouldn't be a problem." Damn, she didn't say that right. "You should know, I didn't tell him anything. I would never—I just meant…he knows *something* happened and you were involved, but he didn't seem to be concerned."

"Even if he were, I'll still pass the vetting. There's no record of anything, and the Pentagon will back me to the end of time. The only time they wouldn't protect me would be if the cover-up fell apart, word got out, and they needed to use me as a scapegoat. But with Gopher dead and Mouse in custody, that isn't going to happen." He brushed her hair off her forehead, his thumb gently grazing the bandaged cut on her brow. "With no record or eyewitness account of what happened in Somalia, I'm in the clear. Dominick can't hold something that never happened against me."

She snuggled back against him.

Keith cleared his throat. "I'm going to tell you what happened in Somalia, but we'll never be able to speak of it again."

"You don't have to—"

"I know. And I appreciate that. But you already know the worst part—the secret. What you don't know is why, and I want you to know the reason I did it." He pulled back. "But the floor isn't the most comfortable... Mind if we move to the bed?"

She rose and then reached out a hand. He took it and stood, then led her to the bedroom.

Under the covers of the bed, he lay on his back, and she curled against his side with her head on his chest. His heart beat a steady cadence. When the silence continued, she stroked the wiry hairs on his chest. "You don't need to tell me. It's okay."

"No. I'm just trying to figure out where to start." He paused. "Somalia was slowly emerging from civil war, but was still a mess of interwarlord, interclan violence. As you know, my SEAL team was there because of a rising al Qaeda leader. It was a reconnaissance mission to determine if the leader could be taken out without triggering further clan warfare. We were based at a camp set up by the UN to protect refugees, displaced by years of civil war. An East African major general named Kassa was the UN force commander. He was in charge of the camp under the UN charter. That was the UN's first mistake. Kassa and his troops were from a neighboring country. Too close, too many unresolved ethnic conflicts."

He closed his eyes, and she waited, saying nothing.

He was reliving something behind those lowered lids, and it was obvious the memory pained him even now.

He cleared his throat. "A few days after we arrived, a warlord, who was supposed to be a UN ally, started rounding up people. Families. Women. Children. The elderly. The boys who hadn't been conscripted into fighting a brutal clan war. They claimed it was relocation, but the refugees were being led to their deaths. They were committing genocide within spitting distance of a UN force. It was Srebrenica all over again."

Trina may be a Cold War expert, but she'd studied the Balkan conflicts. "Srebrenica—you mean when the eight thousand men and boys who were under the protection of Dutch troops were killed."

"Yeah. The Dutch force commander denies he knew they were being led to their deaths, but there are conflicting accounts. The UN couldn't act then—and the same thing was happening again in Somalia. People were dying, and everyone knew it. But we couldn't do anything. It would go against our charter to intervene. Treaties would crumble.

"I conferred with a few of the SEALs—only a few, because we couldn't involve the whole team. This wasn't—couldn't be—a US military op. If we took action to intervene in a genocide being conducted by allies, we had to make it look like vigilante violence. Preferably like the local warlord was behind it.

"Three of us took a Humvee and scouted the area. Tracking the trucks that had taken off with the refugees. We located the death camp and searched the area on foot. We found the leaders and got the shock of our lives. There was Major General Kassa with the warlord. He wasn't just looking the other way because of an international charter. He was actively involved, committing genocide under the auspices of the UN. The enemy wasn't the local warlord. The enemy was us."

Trina couldn't imagine the horror of discovering the UN peacekeeping camp's force commander was directing a wartime atrocity. All she could do was stroke Keith's chest and listen. His arm tightened around her and she was grateful he trusted her enough to share this story. Not because she wanted or needed to know what happened, but because he needed to talk about it and be comforted. Held.

His voice was low, quiet. "If I could have, I'd have shot Kassa right then. But we weren't ready. It was too risky. We needed a plan." He rubbed his face. "A day went by before we were ready.

Another busload of people was carted off. That, more than anything, haunts me. It was selfish of me to hesitate. To wait to take action so I could cover my own ass."

"You weren't covering your ass. You were covering the UN's ass. If it were revealed a UN force commander was part of a genocide—essentially meaning the UN was committing genocide—the organization might never have recovered. And given the chaos that would have ensued in Somalia, you might not have stopped the warlord. It could have gotten worse."

He nodded. "There's knowing that, and there's believing that. I have a hard time with the second one. I just know we waited a day and people died." He took a shuddering breath. "We had to take out the major general while he was inside the camp, but still make it look like an outside job. That required a long shot from outside the fence—as the team sniper, that made the kill my job. We agreed I'd take the shot without Owen as my spotter. It was an alibi of sorts—to have my spotter in the camp instead of with me.

"I used an old Soviet Dragunov rifle that we confiscated from Somali combatants. I was careful with the shells—they'd been handled by the soldiers and likely had sweat that would indicate East African DNA, which would be our 'proof' the shooter had been Somali, not someone of Anglo-Saxon heritage like me. It was weak, but it was the best way we could come up with to cover my ass in the ensuing investigation."

Trina sensed from his tone that was another guilt trigger for him, and caught his hand in hers and gently squeezed his fingers.

"The plan was pretty simple. After I shot the major general, my job was to disappear back into the local village. Owen and Josh would head off in pursuit of the shooter and knowing my position on a low hill east of the camp, find the rifle and casing. I got out fine, but one of the warlord's thugs must have gotten a glimpse of me, because he got to where I'd left the rifle first. Josh said he blindsided Owen with the butt of the Dragunov. Josh shot him. We had our sniper, no need for DNA, but at the cost of Owen."

Trina could see it all in her mind. Owen Bishop, in his prime, recklessly charging the hill, expecting to find nothing but an abandoned gun, and being met with the butt of a rifle to the head.

"When I got back into the camp, Owen was bloody and blue. Medics were performing CPR. We thought he was going to die. The bleeding under his skull was so bad. They had to drill holes to relieve the pressure. He was airlifted to Germany, then later to Bethesda.

"When he was finally conscious, it became clear he didn't remember. It seemed kinder not to tell him—since it was a secret he might reveal. I never dreamed he'd remember the worst part, that I'd killed Kassa, without remembering why. He's had chronic pain. Depression. PTSD. You name it. The guy was severely injured, and he didn't even know why. What if... what if we'd told him? Maybe we could have prevented his problem with addiction."

He carried so much guilt. It was clear he blamed himself for Owen's injury, but also for Owen's difficulty in recovering. Trina's heart ached for the weight Keith carried. "You couldn't have told him while he was still recovering. You've been right all along. This secret is too big. It's not just big... It's colossal. Under the UN charter, American troops led by an American general took the East Africans' place in Somalia. If anyone guessed an American SEAL had shot the East African UN force commander, the fallout would have been enormous. And a man recovering from a brain injury is unreliable. I don't think you could have done anything different."

"I know that. In my head. But it's still my fault. They went after the rifle so no one would suspect me—"

"And them, because they were just as involved, and to protect the UN. You weren't the only one at risk. How many lives did you save? How many did Owen save? Everyone on your team is a hero for the action you all took that day."

"There were five thousand people in the camp. At least two hundred were killed before we intervened."

She stroked his arms, his chest, his stomach. Her touch wasn't much, but it was the only comfort she could offer. "Thanks for telling me."

"I wanted you to know. I did kill the general. And except for what happened to Owen, it's the best thing I've ever done."

CHAPTER EIGHTEEN

A FINGER OF light caressed Trina's hair and cheek. To Keith, it appeared as if the sun had broken into the room, determined to find the most beautiful object to shine upon. He leaned down and kissed the light, kissed her smooth cheek, and gave silent thanks for this moment, for having her not only in his bed but also in his life.

Her eyes fluttered open. She smiled and arched her back in a stretch, then grimaced. "Ugh. The accident caught up with me." She gingerly lifted her arms and straightened her legs, her frown deepening. "I think every part of me is sore."

"We've got an hour before we need to be at the Justice Department. Enough time for me to give you a massage."

Her sleepy eyes opened wider. "Seriously? I could really get into this whole relationship thing if it includes massages first thing in the morning."

He chuckled and nudged her onto her belly, then straddled her butt and dug into her shoulders with his palms and thumbs. She groaned.

They were both naked, and his cock thickened at the sexy noises she made as he worked at the knots below her shoulder blades. His erection rested along the cleft of her butt, and she wiggled, but he was determined to ignore the invitation and give her a selfless massage.

But she kept wiggling. Kept moaning, and he was finding it hard to stay focused on just pleasuring her with massage. One hand slipped lower without his permission, and he scooted back a bit so those wayward fingers could explore her wet opening. She was slick and ready and thrust her butt up, begging. Demanding.

"Get inside me, Keith. *Please.*"

Well, since she said please…

He grabbed a condom from the nightstand, sheathed himself, then spread her thighs and filled her, her round ass pressed against his pelvis as his cock stroked her inside. He resumed the back massage, rubbing her shoulders in time with each thrust.

If he'd thought the noises she'd made while he massaged were sexy, it was nothing compared to the guttural groan she let out as his fingers worked a pressure point and his cock pressed her G-spot. She went from groans to a low, deep moan, followed by a shriek that she couldn't contain as her vagina clenched around him and her body rocked with orgasm.

Her tightening around his cock triggered a pulse of pleasure that made him groan. Forgetting the massage, he dropped down and pressed his cheek between her shoulder blades. She clenched again, the sensation so amazing, so frigging hot. He drove into her tight heat. Bliss. He let out a hoarse cry with his release, powerful in spite of the fact that he'd come more than once in the hours before they went to sleep.

"Holy hell, Trina. How do you do this to me?" He kissed her shoulders, breathing her warm scent.

She laughed, and he rose up and slid out of her so she could turn over. He disposed of the condom, then they settled together in the middle of the bed, entwined.

Keith had struggled these last months, defeated by his visit with his father when he'd first left the Navy. His family was lost to him, but he had Josh, Owen, and other members of his team. And now with Trina, he had a chance to create the only family that really mattered.

Ψ

KEITH HELD TRINA'S hand as they entered the Justice Department yet again, and for what Trina hoped would be the final interview. She was ready to put this nightmare behind her and take a few days off so she could explore a future with the warrior who had started off as a work assignment but now was all play.

Inside the government building, they were escorted to Curt and an FBI agent, who stood by a window that overlooked an interrogation room. Vole sat alone at a table in the stark room. They'd just finished exchanging greetings when the Secretary of Homeland Security and deputy attorney general joined them.

"We've made some very disturbing discoveries overnight," Curt began. "It appears Vole and Ruby were in deep with a man we believe is a Chinese spy." He met Trina's gaze. "This morning, we went over the security camera recording from the coffee shop when you met with Ruby—AKA Gopher—and noticed that his gaze wasn't randomly darting around the room as he created the scene. He kept looking at this man." Curt held up a grainy black-and-white photo, which had to be a still shot pulled from the surveillance camera. "Does he look familiar to you, Trina?"

"No. I didn't notice him." She'd been so mortified by Ruby's outburst she'd purposely avoided meeting the gazes of the other patrons in the shop.

"You haven't seen him elsewhere? In your apartment building or on the Metro?"

She shrugged. "Definitely not in my building. I know all the residents. But I could easily have sat next to him on the Metro and wouldn't notice."

"Who is he?" the Secretary of Homeland Security asked.

"From what we've been able to piece together from Ruby's computer, we think his alias is Matthew Ling. As far as we can tell, the real Ling is a software developer who was born in San Francisco and currently resides in Arizona. This man has probably been in the US for six months or so. It doesn't appear Ruby knew the guy was a spy, but the explosion probably tipped him off that his source wasn't the American activist he presented himself to be."

Keith nodded to the window. "What does Vole have to say about Ling?"

"We haven't asked him yet. It's time to find out what he knows." Curt nodded to the secretary. "Wait until he lawyers up, then come in and drop the hammer." Curt and an FBI agent entered the interrogation room, leaving the secretary, the deputy attorney general, Keith, and Trina outside to watch through the window.

Vole's eyes widened as he tucked himself into a ball. Then he seemed to remember himself and straightened. Defiant. "You can't kill me like you did Gopher. If you don't let me go, my story about the US Navy's assassination of a UN force commander in Somalia will run on the website. Major General Kassa was killed so a US general could take his place, securing UN power firmly with the United States. The assassination was covered up by the Pentagon and made to look like a local warlord did the killing, but it was a SEAL team op. The US military's actions need to be exposed. The people have a right to know when tax dollars are used to assassinate foreign military leaders. They have a right to know when there has been a coup within the UN."

"Don't waste my time with stupid threats. Our computer forensics team has already broken through your security. It doesn't matter that the site is hosted outside the US. All we needed was your and Ruby's access codes to get the site pulled. I employ the best in the business, and once we had your computers, cracking your codes was a snap. RATinformant is down. For good."

The light in Derrick's eyes shifted. He looked strangely gleeful for someone backed into a corner and facing a host of federal charges, including espionage and murder.

"If you're feeling smug because of your hydra program, rest assured, my hacker found and destroyed that before taking the site off-line. RATinformant can no longer replicate and upload. It's gone. For good."

The hope in Derrick's eyes faded.

"Why did you go after Dr. Sorensen?" Curt asked.

"She knew what happened in Somalia. We got the junkie out of rehab. He still wouldn't tell us, but we knew he'd tell her. He was burning to tell someone. She had clearance and authorization. She was the opportunity he'd been waiting for to spill his guts and release his guilt over murdering a major general."

Keith's gaze dropped, and she knew it must hurt to hear Owen's condition spoken of in such callous terms. This morning, Keith had talked to Owen's aunt, who was distraught to learn she'd been manipulated into calling the rehab center. Knowing Owen's treatment had been ruined so Trina could interview him was an especially bitter pill. She'd played right into their hands.

"I'd been following Bishop and knew he had met with her. I called Gopher to tell him Bishop had just left the DOJ. Dr. Sorensen had the information, and I'd intercept her when she left the building. But while we were on the phone, he bit it."

"So you're claiming you didn't kill your partner?" The FBI agent asked.

Vole bristled. "Hell no! That was you murdering government thugs!"

"Sorry. But it wasn't us," Curt said. "We wanted him alive so we could question him and were gathering data for a warrant."

Vole jumped to his feet, and Trina realized he'd been shackled to the floor. He couldn't pace; he could only stand. He jolted back into his chair. "Bullshit. Since when does the government wait for a warrant? Ever since the Patriot Act—"

"Mr. Vole, you can save your speeches for your fellow cell-mates. I don't have time." Curt leaned forward and fixed the man with a piercing stare. "We found evidence in Brian Ruby's apartment that connects him to the bomb in Dr. Sorensen's laptop. Can you explain that?"

Surprise hit Trina in the gut. Curt hadn't told her that. She'd figured Ruby had to be the one, but there was some relief in knowing.

Vole flopped backward in his seat. "I want a lawyer."

The FBI agent grinned. "Why? If it was Ruby who planted the bomb, you have nothing to lose by talking to us. He'll take the fall, and conveniently for you, he's dead."

Vole wasn't really going to fall for that was he? But he surprised Trina and leaned forward, his mouth open, as if he intended to keep talking. Then his jaw snapped shut.

Silence stretched out. Finally, the Secretary of Homeland Security said, "That was my cue," and left the observation room. A moment later, he stepped into the interrogation room. He introduced himself to the nervous suspect and flashed a cunning smile. "We have evidence, Mr. Vole, that you published stories which seriously jeopardized national security. Furthermore, the fabrication about Somalia you intended to make public on your website could undermine US standing in the United Nations and even bring down NATO."

The secretary's words hung in the air, and Trina caught her breath at the enormity of the situation. If any version of what happened got out, the only way for the US to salvage their role in the UN would be for Keith to take the fall, to claim he acted on his own and the cover-up was his own. The members of his SEAL team would have to do the same. They'd all face charges of treason. Even execution.

So, yeah. When Keith said he couldn't talk about Somalia, he'd meant it.

"Furthermore, the US could face retaliation from African nations if such a story were to come to light. For these reasons, Homeland Security and the FBI have deemed you an enemy combatant. The regular rules regarding the Fifth Amendment and Miranda rights are suspended. We can hold you indefinitely."

Vole glared at the secretary. "This is a sham, and labeling me an enemy combatant is only going to make my fellow daylight-law activists more eager to uncover your lies. We still have freedom of the press in this country."

"Freedom of the press?" the secretary said. "You're going to try that angle? That won't fly when word gets out that you actively passed classified information to a foreign spy. That's not reporting, Mr. Vole, that's espionage. And that's exactly what you'll be charged with.

"And I have good news for you. You're about to have front-row center seats in a secret court—the very type of trial you've been so eager to expose to the world on your website. Perhaps after going through the process, you will finally understand the need to keep some things within the government a secret."

"Spy? What the hell are you talking about?"

Curt slapped the surveillance camera photo on the table. "If you want to avoid Guantanamo Bay, you'd better tell me everything you know about this man right now, starting with why he made Ruby plant a bomb in Dr. Sorensen's laptop."

CHAPTER NINETEEN

VOLE FELL APART when Dominick threatened him with Gitmo, and the bastard started talking. Keith watched with rapt attention as Vole claimed he'd never met Ling face-to-face, but Ruby had a few times. Vole communicated with Ling via different e-mail accounts and physical drops of documents in various locations inside the Beltway.

According to Vole, the idea of planting the Somalia assignment in an NHHC historian's computer came about after he started working on the campaign event with Dr. Hill's assistant and the joint project between NHHC and the MacLeod-Hill Institute was mentioned several times. Vole researched the various historians and selected Walt Fryer because his clearance level was high and his pay grade even higher than that of the interim director. Because of his seniority, he had several projects that came directly from the Pentagon, bypassing Mara Garrett's approval.

Ruby contacted Fryer ostensibly to discuss the UN coalition post-Desert Storm and used the opportunity to upload the assignment directly into Fryer's computer. The e-mail had all the right codes; it had just never followed the expected trail from Pentagon to NHHC.

When Fryer didn't jump on the assignment, Ruby contacted him to set up another appointment, intending to plant another e-mail to nudge him along. But he brushed off Ruby, saying Trina would handle the assignment from that point forward, that she handled all of his assignments that weren't related to World War II.

A tap on Keith's shoulder startled him, and he looked away from the interrogation happening on the other side of the two-way mirror and recognized the FBI analyst who had initially been assigned to work on Keith's background check, but who was now combing through his dad's e-mails, which they'd managed to rescue from the cloud backup of Keith's hard drive, searching for a connection to RATinformant.

The look on the analyst's face caused yet another wave of dread. Just when Keith thought his father couldn't hurt him anymore, the son of a bitch found a way.

He left the observation room, following the analyst into the hall. Keith didn't bother to waste time with pleasantries. "What did you find?"

"I'm sorry, Hatcher, but it looks like your dad is Muskrat. There was language he used in several e-mails he sent you six weeks ago that is nearly verbatim what Muskrat posted on RATinformant two weeks ago. There are too many similarities in word choices and syntax—even when the topic is different—to be a fluke. Plus the posts on the site don't appear to be Muskrat quoting someone else. It's the same man."

Christ, the same method that had identified the Unabomber had caught his dad. And if Keith had bothered to read his father's crazy e-mails or search the Internet for his ranting posts, he would have known. Maybe he even could have prevented everything that had happened. His dad had to be the one who told Vole that Owen was in rehab, and his dad knew just enough about Keith's SEAL team to have convinced Owen's trusting aunt to talk to Vole.

"Is he going to be arrested today?" Keith asked.

"The San Francisco special agent in charge is working on a warrant right now."

"Let the agents who serve the warrant know he's armed to the teeth, and he's a crack shot. He was my first firearms instructor. I'm afraid he won't be taken peacefully."

The analyst nodded. "We figured that from his Muskrat posts. And with the site down, he might have guessed we've identified him."

A knot clenched Keith's gut. "Tell the SAC they need to grab him when he's away from his stockpile of weapons. I might be able to get one of my brothers to draw him out."

Trina stepped out of the interrogation observation room and took Keith's hand. The analyst said he'd pass on the information and left them alone.

She gazed up at him, concern in her beautiful hazel eyes. He didn't say a word, just pulled her to his chest and held her tight.

☨

TRINA RETURNED TO the interrogation observation room in time to witness Vole's account of how Ruby planted the explosive in her laptop.

They planned carefully, knowing Dr. Hill's party had the potential to give Trina an opportunity to talk to Keith, if she hadn't been able to chase him down already. Vole was there to orchestrate a meeting if need be. More important, once the assignment fell to Trina, Ling had been concerned her research on Somalia would be questioned—in a way it wouldn't be if Walt had kept the assignment. The e-mails that appeared to be from the Pentagon would never hold up under deep scrutiny. Ling insisted Ruby needed to plant a virus in Trina's computer that would destroy the NHHC e-mail server, along with a flash bomb that would destroy her computer after the virus uploaded, thus destroying the trail completely.

They determined the best time to place the explosive would be while Trina attended the party at Hill's. Vole's job was to call Ruby if she left early, so she wouldn't walk in on him while he hacked her computer. From Vole's account, it sounded as if both he and Ruby had become afraid of Ling and had come to suspect he was a spy. He knew their names and addresses, and the names and addresses of their extended family members. If they didn't do what he wanted, he could out them as RATs at any time.

Knowing they faced charges for posting classified documents online that included the names of Syrian informants who'd provided information to the UN during their ongoing civil war, and the Syrian government had then rounded up those informants and executed them, Ruby and Vole did what Ling wanted. Ruby planted the explosive.

All had gone according to plan, except Keith's apartment blew up instead of just Trina's computer, and the blast had told Ruby and Vole that the explosive Ling had provided was far more powerful than simple thermite. Ruby had freaked.

Ling told Ruby the reason for the stronger explosive was to take out Walt's computer, one cubicle over, which held the initial e-mails about Somalia, but both Ruby and Vole knew from that point forward that Ling had an objective that went a far step beyond RATinformant's daylight-law philosophy.

Vole said Ruby considered turning himself in, but decided to meet with Trina first, hoping she could help him cut a deal with the attorney general. Except minutes before the meeting, Ling cornered him and warned him not to say anything. Then Ling set himself up in the coffee shop and monitored Ruby. Ruby's hostility was a show to let Ling know he was toeing the line.

It appeared Ling had killed Ruby anyway, because Ruby had been prepared to turn himself in, and he was the only person who had seen Ling's face.

Trina rubbed her temples, her head aching as she took in how thoroughly she'd been manipulated. She bumped her glasses, and for the fourth time in the last hour, the lens popped out of the cracked frame.

Beyond the two-way mirror, Curt ended the interview with Vole, then stepped into the observation area. He sent the Secretary of Homeland Security and deputy attorney general to wait in his office, then asked Trina and Keith to meet with him in the conference room where she'd interviewed Owen the previous afternoon.

They gathered in the room, and Curt's gaze landed on Trina. She knew him well enough to see the concern in his eyes. "Trina, you're going to have to stay at the safe house indefinitely. As long as Ling is at large, you're in danger."

She'd expected this, but it was frightening nonetheless. "What about Keith?"

Keith dropped an arm around her shoulders, hugging her to his side.

"Keith too." Curt smiled. "You can stay together—but Keith, no more extracurricular ops. I'll expect you to stay put."

Now it was Keith's turn to smile. He stood at attention and said a crisp, "Yes, sir."

She laughed. Well, at least she was going into hiding *with* Keith. And with the right stilettos and underwear, life in the safe house could be fun. "Can I return to my place long enough to pack a bag? My glasses are broken. I need to grab another pair." And there were those knee-high boots she'd been wanting an excuse to wear.

"Sure. I have agents there right now, so it's safe. I just need to find someone to take you there, then deliver you to the safe house." He fixed a gaze on Keith. "You can't take her. I need you to talk to the SAC in San Francisco."

"Understood. Rav called Sean in to guard Trina. He's here now and can take her."

Curt nodded. "Good." Then he reached out and hugged her. "We're going to do everything we can to round up Ling quickly. If we don't have him in the next twenty-four hours through covert leads, we're going public. Make no mistake, public or not, Ling currently tops the FBI's most wanted list."

She nodded. "Thanks, Curt."

"I'll give you two a moment. Keith, meet me in my office when you're done."

Keith nodded.

The moment Curt left, Keith opened his arms, and Trina stepped into them. He'd suffered a blow learning his dad was actively involved with RATinformant, and she ached for him.

"The only thing that's getting me through this day is knowing you and I will be home together tonight." He cradled her face. "I love you, Trina. I feel awful you were dragged in to this. It's my fault you're in danger and being forced to hide. But I'm selfishly grateful to have you."

"If there is anyone to blame, it's the dammed UN force commander. You did the right thing in Somalia, and you aren't responsible for what your father has done." She could see he wasn't ready to relinquish guilt, but she had all the time in the world to work on that with him. She kissed him and said, "I love you, and I'm selfishly grateful to have you too." She flashed a wicked smile. "Since I'm going home to pack, tell me, do you prefer garters or a teddy?"

"Which one of us is going to wear it?"

She choked on a laugh. "Now that you mention it…"

He kissed her, then said, "I prefer you in nothing at all and think you're sexy in everything. Surprise me."

She had a wide, sappy grin on her face as she and Sean set out for her apartment. It was late afternoon. Keith expected to be able to join her at the safe house in an hour or two. There were worse things than being forced to go into hiding with a hot former SEAL.

When they arrived at her apartment, the FBI agents were just packing up and leaving. They'd been looking for signs anyone besides Ruby had broken in and searched the place. Cressida had been called in to provide fingerprints for elimination purposes, and they'd contacted her boyfriend, Todd, in Tallahassee and instructed him to submit prints to the Jacksonville Field Office.

Every surface of her home was coated in black powder. Well, at least this mess wasn't her fault. Deep down she figured the search for fingerprints was a futile effort. Ruby had worn gloves, and if Ling had been here, he'd have worn gloves as well.

A nervous ache clenched her belly. As fun as it would be to play house with Keith, she couldn't help but wonder how long it would take before the powers that be would determine she had to go into deep hiding, never to return to her previous life and the job that she loved?

Sean must have guessed her thoughts from the way she frowned as she took in the mess, because he said, "They'll find him, Trina. Or they'll find proof he fled the country."

"I hope so."

She grabbed a cloth and began cleaning the residue from the counter, but Sean stopped her. "We can't stay long enough for you to clean. Pack a bag, and we're out of here. You can hire a cleaning service to take care of the mess."

She nodded and told herself to suck it up. Keith had lost everything when his home blew up. For her to whine about a little powder was ridiculous. She marched into her bedroom to pack. Sean followed at her heels.

He was a nice man, but having a bodyguard was stifling.

From her overstuffed closet she passed over the small overnight bag and grabbed the bigger suitcase tucked into the back. She placed it on the bed and pulled the zipper, which snagged at the second corner. With a tug, she heard a pop, and it broke free.

A hissing sound caught her attention as she flipped the top open. Sean lunged forward. "Don't!"

The last thing she saw was the cloud of white gas that poured from the suitcase.

Ψ

KEITH'S CELL PHONE buzzed. He glanced down, and his stomach dropped. Sean had hit the panic button on his phone.

He bolted to his feet, interrupting the meeting of bigwigs he'd been silently observing. "Trina's in trouble. Sean hit the panic button on his cell phone." Keith's mind was already racing. The panic button was an app signal that went out to all Raptor operatives in the area, including Rav.

Keith dialed Rav even as he walked out of Dominick's office, abandoning the meeting. The attorney general was at his heels, his own cell phone to his ear.

Rav answered immediately. "Where is Sean?" he asked without preamble.

"He took Trina to her apartment."

Next to him, Dominick was speaking urgently into his phone. "You left? Go back. Now. She's in trouble." To Keith, he said, "The agents who were searching her place had finished. They left right after Trina and Sean arrived."

Keith made a beeline for the exit. "I'm heading over."

"I'm coming with you," Dominick said. He followed Keith outside to his car, making calls and giving orders as he went. "I need an emergency unit en route to Dr. Sorensen's apartment, now! I'm riding with Hatcher, and I want full updates of all radio dispatches. I'll keep this line open."

Keith's brain had switched into full combat mode as he slipped behind the wheel of his borrowed SUV. He had to compartmentalize. He couldn't think in terms of Trina being in danger. This was an op. Every op had two objectives: take out the target, and protect his brothers-in-arms. Like every op, there was only one acceptable outcome.

CHAPTER TWENTY

THE FIRST SENSATION Trina felt was fierce pain behind her eyes. Enough to make her want to retreat back into sleep or whatever state of consciousness she'd been in. She twitched, and the movement triggered sudden, violent nausea.

She turned her head to the side on instinct alone and tossed up her lunch. Her head felt as if it would split with each convulsive heave. Cold sweat dampened her skin.

She must have some sort of stomach bug. A bad one. Where was she? A hospital?

With effort, she opened her eyes. Sunlight caused another jabbing pain.

Not a hospital. Not even inside a building. She was in a car. Bound in the backseat. She'd just vomited on the floor. All she could see through the window was sunshine and sky.

Where was she going? Who had taken her?

She couldn't see the driver from her vantage point right behind the driver's seat. As far as she could tell, she was the vehicle's only passenger.

Where was Keith? No. Not Keith. Sean. She'd been with Sean in her apartment, hadn't she?

The memory came back—opening the suitcase, the gas. Then nothing until now.

Again she looked out the window. City buildings came into view. She was still in DC. In blessed stop-and-go traffic.

She eyed the door handle, wondering if she could open it and roll out before the driver could react. Her hands seemed to be bound, but maybe with her feet?

"You're awake," an unfamiliar voice said. "Don't bother trying the door. Child locks." There was a slight accent to his voice that suggested an Asian background, confirming her fear. She'd been taken by Ling.

She tried to sit up, then discovered she'd been shackled—zip-tied, from the feel of the plastic at her wrists—to the metal child car seat latch next to the seat-belt buckle. With her arms behind her back, her range of motion was limited. Her ankles were bound together but not tethered like her arms.

She had no clue where this man was taking her, but odds were it wouldn't end well for her if they reached his intended destination. Alone, he'd be in complete control.

She pulled her knees to her chest, ignoring the sharp jabs of pain every motion triggered inside her skull, and kicked at the window. She couldn't quite reach.

Being short sucks.

She scooted downward, even though it meant torqueing her arms. Pain burned along her shoulder joint, but her heels hit the window. The rubber soles of her running shoes bounced on the glass.

The car swerved as the driver realized what she was doing. He said something sharply in what sounded to her untrained ears like Chinese. In English, he said, "I will shoot you if you try that again."

She was dead when they arrived at their destination anyway. She kicked again. And again. On the fourth kick, the window shattered, safety glass rained down and out, and she screamed with all her energy for help, hoping the noise would rise above the traffic, that someone driving with their window down on the hot summer afternoon would hear her.

The muzzle of a pistol appeared in the gap between the driver and passenger seats. "Stop screaming."

She took a deep breath and let out a scream that eclipsed the others, and braced herself for the gun to fire.

But it didn't. Whoever this man was, he'd risked a lot to take her alive. They were probably headed someplace where he planned to torture the truth about Somalia out of her.

She kicked forward, hoping to dislodge the weapon, but missed. She had no leverage in that direction, tethered as she was to her side. All she could do was scream and flail her bound feet, hoping someone would hear and see her legs and alert the police.

And so she did. She screamed for all she was worth. This could be her only chance.

The gun fired, going high and into the seat cushion above her hips. Either he couldn't aim while facing forward and driving with one hand, or he'd missed on purpose.

Surely the sound of the gunshot would have gotten someone's attention on the city street.

Sirens sounded in the distance, then grew louder.

Please, let that be the cavalry.

The car lurched to a stop. The driver jerked open his door. Was he leaving her?

No such luck. The door by her head wrenched open, and there was her abductor—the man from the surveillance camera photo— lunging toward her with a knife. She cringed, closing her eyes as the blade sliced toward her.

Her hands popped free—he'd used the blade on the zip-tie, nicking her skin but cutting the circle that looped her wrists. She didn't hesitate and scratched at him. He yanked her hair, pulling her from the vehicle. She spilled out onto the city street, feet still bound.

He sliced the zip-tie around her ankles. She tried to scramble up on all fours in spite of the pain of shooting pins and needles. He caught her again by her hair, dislodging her glasses, which fell to the pavement. He yanked her to her feet. The blade dropped and was replaced by the gun, which he thrust against her temple.

Panic filled her mouth with a metallic taste.

The world was a blur, her senses jumbled, and not just because her vision was poor beyond five feet. Cars were coming to a screeching halt on the street. Sirens, shouts, fear, and being jerked about by Ling had her in sensory overload.

She took a deep breath and tried to get her bearings. Squinting, she saw a park before them. Ling dragged her toward a statue in the center. She recognized the statue. Farragut Square.

Innocent bystanders stood between her and Ling and the statue. She screamed, yelling at them to clear the way. Mothers grabbed their babies and ran. A jogger stopped to help an elderly woman who stood frozen on the path. Ling pulled Trina relentlessly forward.

They reached the statue. Ling jumped the low fence and pulled her over. The metal bar that topped the fence scraped her spine. He scaled the three steps and pressed his back against a corner stone, holding her in front of him. She was a human shield.

Ling had made a final play to get the story of what happened in Somalia from her, but a driver who witnessed her struggle must have forced him from the road. Now he was trapped. There was no scenario she could imagine in which he would escape without keeping her as his hostage.

More emergency vehicles piled up on the roadway as traffic stopped in all directions. The park was cleared in a matter of minutes.

The gun pressed against her temple as Ling made sounds she assumed were Chinese curses. His hands shook.

There was no way her government would let him go, even with her as a hostage. Without a miracle, her life was forfeit.

CHAPTER TWENTY-ONE

DOMINICK AND KEITH arrived within moments of the first officers. Keith watched as Trina was dragged to the statue and the man held her before him as cover.

Dominick's phone was pressed to his ear as he shouted questions. But this was now an FBI hostage situation, which wasn't Dominick's specialty.

"I'm going to take him out," Keith said to Dominick, then reached for the rear hatch of the SUV.

"You've got a rifle?"

He gave a quick nod and grabbed the case from the back. He scanned the area, looking for a good vantage point, where he could see Ling, but Ling wouldn't know he was in his sights.

That parked car or that thick tree would do.

"You can't, Hatcher—"

"I can and I will."

"An FBI hostage negotiator will be here in minutes."

He fixed Dominick with a hard stare. "You and I both know we can't let Ling escape with Trina. She'll never stand up to torture. And after he gets what he wants, he'll kill her anyway. There can't be a negotiation."

"You can't be the one to take this shot. Not when he's using Trina as a shield."

"I'm the *only* one who can take this shot, *because* he's using Trina as a shield. Do you think I could trust anyone else with her life?" *What if someone else fucks up and hits Trina?* He'd…he couldn't even consider it. "I will take him out. No one but me."

Dominick must have heard something in his tone, because he gave a quick nod. Or he was simply living up to his reputation as a chess player and read the board as well as Keith had. They were short on time. They couldn't wait for another sniper, and Keith was here, with a rifle. Ready and willing.

He set up the M110 by rote. He cleared his mind by focusing

on the only details that mattered now. Distance of the shot. Size of the target. An American flag on top of the building behind the statue gave him the wind direction, but it was too high to give him a good idea of wind speed at ground level. The leaves on the tree before him fluttered slightly. Light wind on a humid day.

He rested the barrel in the V of a tree branch, adjusted the scope, and used Trina's known height to gauge the distance to the target. He dialed in, and her wide, scared eyes appeared in the crosshairs. He shifted immediately. No.

Don't think. Do your job.

Four square inches of Ling's face was visible above and behind Trina's. A small target. But he'd made the same shot from a greater distance many times. This was what he trained for. This was what he did.

Strands of brown hair flashed in the circle of the sights, then disappeared. Trina's hair. Her head was that close to his target. Agitated, Ling shifted, pulling Trina with him. Both their heads bobbed in the crosshairs.

Suddenly, Trina stilled.

Yes, babe. I'm out here. Don't move, and I will take him out.

He placed the center a mil above Ling's right eye. He took a slow breath, aware of his heartbeat. Habit. Training. This was where it all came together. He pulled the trigger, slowly, mindful to keep the release just as soft.

Blood splattered the statue behind Trina, and Ling fell to the ground.

⊕

THE MOMENT LING'S arms went slack, Trina ran forward, jumping over the low fence. She didn't look behind her, didn't know if he was dead or if his gun was aimed at her back. She didn't care. She just ran.

She heard a shout—Keith's voice—and turned in that direction. She recognized the way he moved even without her glasses. He caught her in his arms and held her against his firm chest. "Babe," he whispered over and over again.

She wrapped her arms around his waist and held him tight. She would collapse if she let go. Finally, she found her voice. "What happened to Sean? Is he okay?"

"He's fine. He was bound and gagged in your apartment. He

came to right as FBI agents smashed through the door. He said you'd both been gassed. A minute after that, reports of a woman kicking out a window and screaming bloody murder on Seventeenth Street came over the police scanner, and that another driver had run him off the road."

"It wasn't Sean's fault. He searched my apartment before I went into my bedroom. No one was there. The gas—"

"I know. The same thing would have happened if it had been me who took you there, but I might not have been quick like Sean and hit the panic button before passing out. With the FBI having just been there, we were too confident it was safe."

Once again Trina found herself pulled away from Keith to be checked over by a paramedic. The FBI was running tests to determine what gas had been used, but the effects at least appeared to be temporary, probably thanks to the fact that Ling— or whatever his name was—had needed to take her alive.

They returned to the DOJ, but Trina insisted on riding with Keith. She was done with the being-questioned-separately bullshit.

They gathered in Curt's office. Swaddled in a thick, plush blanket, she sat on a couch and leaned on Keith instead of taking a seat in front of Curt's desk.

They would probably never know who Ling was exactly. All they knew was he'd been in the US for at least six months, and in that time, he'd thoroughly manipulated two daylight-law activists into spying on their own country for him, managed to get a bomb planted in a computer that was supposed to detonate inside a building on a US Navy base in the nation's capital, and he would have succeeded in abducting Trina and probably torturing the Somalia story from her if she hadn't kicked out the window and made a scene before they got on the bridge and left the city.

Curt left them in his office to confer with the various department heads who had descended on the DOJ after the shooting of a Chinese spy in the heart of DC.

Alone with Keith, she shifted to his lap. They had no reason to suspect anyone was following her. With Ruby's and Ling's deaths, and Vole's capture, the story of a UN force commander's assassination by a Navy SEAL would go nowhere.

Keith's father had surrendered peacefully when he was approached at a grocery store. They'd been told he'd broken down in sobs when he saw the recording of Trina's abduction and

Keith's shot that saved her. He said he only knew the other RATinformants by their avatars and had no idea they'd been working with a spy. Keith was inclined to believe him, so Trina did as well, but regardless, his dad was facing prosecution as an enemy combatant. The man would never be able to spread stories about Somalia even if he was still so inclined.

As for Trina, she would never reveal what she'd learned. She was bound to the same code of silence as Keith's SEAL team and the highest levels of the US military and government. Some secrets were worth keeping—in this instance knowledge was not power.

The only weak link was Owen Bishop. Josh had been successful in getting him back into rehab, and Keith and the rest of his SEAL team would watch out for him. They would do everything they could to help him beat the addiction and find his way back to the land of the living. There were no promises of success, but there was hope.

Trina stroked Keith's stubbly cheek. "So, now that this is all over, you appear to be homeless."

Keith smiled and pressed his nose in her hair. She loved the way he did that. "Not homeless. Tyler's family rented a place in Annandale. When his mom called to say thanks for the gifts you sent, she offered me a room."

She frowned. "Annandale's almost on top of the Beltway. Pretty far out."

His fingertip gently stroked her eyebrow, then circled down to her cheekbone, finally tracing her lips. "Not much farther than Falls Church."

"Yes, but Falls Church is at least near a Metro station."

Keith smiled. "And this is a problem why?"

"Well, you see, I don't have a car. I couldn't visit you there. And I'd like to visit you. Often."

Keith's grin turned bone-meltingly sexy. "I'd like that. I can think of another problem with Annandale. A seven-year-old in the house means no spontaneous sex in the living room. And I really like spontaneous sex in the living room."

Trina felt a little dizzy just remembering the orgasm he'd given her in the living room last night. She liked thinking about that much more than what had happened in Farragut Square. "Well, if you take the job with Raptor, you'll be working near the White House. And I happen to have an apartment centrally located in the city. Convenient to both the Dupont Circle and U Street Metro stations."

"Before you invite me to live with you, shouldn't you check with your roommate?"

"I thought you knew Cressida is only temporary—her internship ends on Friday. She heads back to Tallahassee this weekend."

"Well, then, this *is* an intriguing offer you've presented. A two-bedroom apartment, centrally located, and you. What's the rent?" He winked as he asked the question.

"Three orgasms a day. If you give me four, I'll even throw in meals."

He threw back his head and laughed. "How about we split the rent and food bill and you'll still get four orgasms."

"Promises, promises."

He pulled her snug against him and dropped a light kiss on her lips. "Plus I'll throw in that I'm willing to try to not be such a neat freak if you promise to try to organize a bit."

"What makes you think I need to organize?" Yeah, she tended toward clutter, but how did he know that?

He nipped her bottom lip. "I've seen your office. And I've yet to see you enter a room without dropping everything you're carrying right by the door. The laptop at my place. Shopping bags in the hotel. Your clothes last night—although that met with my full approval. You are always welcome to strip for me when you get home."

His lips moved to her neck, and she felt lovely chills as he nibbled along her sensitive skin. "If I have to clean up my messes, it sounds like living together is going to be more work than sex."

"Probably. But worth it, I think."

She nodded as she closed her eyes, envisioning what it would be like to share a home with Keith, hours spent reading, talking, and making love. She grinned at the mental picture and said, "I can't wait until you organize my library."

THANK YOU

THANK YOU FOR reading *Withholding Evidence*. I hope you enjoyed it!

If you'd like to know when my next book is available, you can sign up for my new release e-mail list at www.Rachel-Grant.net. You can also like my Facebook page at www.facebook.com/RachelGrantAuthor or follow me on Twitter at @RachelSGrant. I'm on Goodreads at www.goodreads.com/RachelGrantAuthor, where you can see what I'm reading and post reviews.

ACKNOWLEDGEMENTS

I'D LIKE TO thank post-apocalyptic/thriller author and US Navy veteran Steven Konkoly for his willingness to answer even the most mundane questions about the US Navy and naval actions in the Balkans and Somalia over the last two decades. Also, thanks for providing a key piece of information at just the right moment, which helped this story take shape. The information Steven provided on UN Peacekeeping operations was correct; all inaccuracies in my fiction are entirely my fault.

Thank you to the plot bunnies, Darcy Burke, Elisabeth Naughton, and Joan Swan, who helped me kick-start the writing of this story.

Thank you to the fabulous authors who critiqued this book: Darcy Burke, Krista Hall, Erica Ridley, and Bria Quinlan. Thank you so much to my wonderful agent, Elizabeth Winick Rubinstein, for your valuable feedback and insight into the story. Huge thanks to my editor, Linda Ingmanson, for helping make this story shine.

Thanks to the NW Pixie Chicks, for another great retreat and for being the best author support group and friends any author could ask for.

To my blogmates at KissandThrill.com, thank you for putting up with me. Thanks also to the secret indie Facebook group, who also put up with me.

Thank you to my children, who mostly put up with me. I love you both with the power of a thousand suns times infinity.

Thank you to my husband, David Grant, who worked in the underwater archaeology branch of Naval History and Heritage Command (back when it was called the Naval Historical Center). Without his insight, this book would be very different. Also I must thank him for the plotting help and for being willing to read and give feedback even though I am not as graceful at taking feedback from him as I am from others. I am so lucky to have you. I love you.

Read on for a preview of

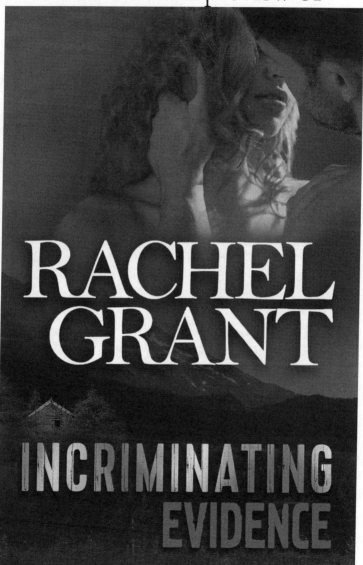

RACHEL GRANT

INCRIMINATING EVIDENCE

From enemies to allies...

When archaeologist Isabel Dawson stumbles upon an unconscious man deep in the Alaskan wilderness, her survival skills are put to the test. She tends his wounds and drags him to shelter, only to discover she's saved the life of Raptor CEO Alec Ravissant—the man who may have covered up her brother's murder to save his senatorial campaign.

With no memory of the assault that landed him five miles deep in the forest, Alec doesn't know what to believe when he wakes in the clutches of the beautiful redhead who blames him for her brother's death, but he quickly realizes he needs her help to uncover the truth about his lost hours.

Isabel never imagined she'd find herself allied with Alec, and he's the last man she ever expected to find attractive. But the former Army Ranger-turned-politician proves seductively charming, and he's determined to win much more than her vote. When their quest for answers puts Isabel in the crosshairs, Alec must risk everything—his company, his campaign, and his life—to protect her.

CHAPTER ONE

Tanana Valley State Forest, Alaska
September

IT WAS A show tunes kind of afternoon, which was unusual for Isabel, but the words to the old songs came to her effortlessly as she walked downslope, deep in the Tanana Valley State Forest. Loud, full-voiced singing was necessary to warn bears she was hiking in this remote Alaskan wilderness and was intended to scare the creatures away. Given her off-key voice, singing pretty much guaranteed humans would stay away as well. A decided bonus.

Although, now that she was on day four of the timber sale survey, she was ready to be done. She'd had enough solitude this week and wouldn't mind meeting up with Nicole for a beer at the Tamarack Roadhouse. It was getting late, already after five p.m., and she was still a two-hour hike from her truck, but her extra-long lunch excursion put her behind schedule and she had one more parcel to inspect before she'd be done with the archaeological survey. It was worth the long day to avoid hiking all the way back here tomorrow.

Most of this week's survey soundtrack had been sad songs, but yesterday had been Vincent's birthday, so her melancholy was understandable. Then suddenly, this afternoon Rodgers and Hammerstein popped into her head. She'd started with *Oklahoma!,* continued with *The Sound of Music,* and now she'd moved on to Gilbert and Sullivan's *The Pirates of Penzance,* specifically, "I Am The Very Model Of A Modern Major-General."

She'd feel ridiculous singing at the top of her lungs, except after months of working in Alaska, she'd grown used to the need to make noise while conducting pedestrian survey. She'd found straight-up talking to herself disconcerting, so she'd taken to singing. Now it was second nature. She barely even heard her own voice as she studied the ground for telltale signs of prehistoric human activity.

She paused, taking a deep breath, preparing for the next rapid verse, when she heard a branch crack, followed by a grunt.

Not the grunt of an animal, but one of a human. In pain?

She stopped. With her head cocked toward the wind, she listened. Again she heard a sound. Faint. Human. Definitely not happy.

She scanned the woods. The underbrush was thick and mosquitoes vicious. Whenever she stopped walking, they swarmed. She fought the urge to wave her arms to shoo them away so she could listen.

But all she heard was wind. Birds. Buzzing mosquitoes as the bloodsucking females feasted on her cheeks and arms. Normal forest sounds.

She slapped away the biters. Maybe she'd heard a wolverine. Their grunts could easily be mistaken for human. Shaking off the foolish notion she'd cross paths with another person out here on the edge of the bush, she resumed walking and singing, but the happy beat was lost. Now she sang solely to ward off bears. She scanned the ground as she walked, looking for signs of prehistoric occupation or use. Her job was to find archaeological sites that would be destroyed by the coming timber harvest. That was what she was here for. She needed to focus on what paid the bills.

The ground sloped at a grade above fifteen percent. Poor conditions for finding a site, because the ground was too steep for occupation. If there were a site in the vicinity, she'd find it at the base of the slope. She continued in that direction, determined to do a good job for her employer, the Alaska Department of Natural Resources.

Branches snapped below her, to the right.

She stopped signing midword.

Any number of fauna could have triggered it. She hadn't seen any scat, at least nothing fresh and therefore worrisome, for the last half mile. But still, she dropped a hand to the grip of her pistol while the other grabbed the bear spray. Of the two, the pistol was the least effective, but the noises had her on edge. While a pistol wasn't good defense against a bear, it was excellent for dealing with humans.

These woods, remote, abundant with resources, yet marginally accessible due to logging roads, could be a gateway to the bush for people on the run. Maybe she'd been foolish to brush off the noise as a wolverine.

Another sound carried on the breeze, and she ducked behind a tree to listen and wait. In her gut, she knew she wasn't about to face down a bear. She held the gun in front of her, pointed upward, clasped between both hands like a prayer. Her heart pounded, but she had no real understanding of why. This just didn't feel *right.*

She couldn't stay behind a tree gripping a gun forever and eased out from her feeble hiding spot. Slowly, silently, she crept down the hillside toward whatever—or whoever—had made the sounds.

She spotted him immediately. Sunlight filtered between the leaves, highlighting the red splatter of blood that covered the man's face. He lay still. Unconscious or dead?

She'd heard of archaeologists finding bodies on survey before, but the accounts always had the earmark of urban myths—two people removed from the teller of the tale. She'd never met anyone who'd actually encountered a corpse themselves. She supposed she'd considered how scary such a find would be, but hadn't really thought beyond that, because really, it just didn't happen.

It was like planning for a head-on collision. She'd been certain that sort of thing would never happen to *her.* Car accidents, kidnappings, tornados, and random bodies in the woods were all on the list of things that happened to other people.

And yet here she was. Adrenaline flooded, frozen with shock, and facing a body in the deep, bear-infested woods.

Her past speculation had been wrong. It wasn't scary; it was utterly terrifying. Worse than facing down a bear, a pair of rattlesnakes, and a brown recluse all at the same time. Nature, she could handle. This wasn't nature.

This was murder.

She glanced left and right. She would never hear anyone approaching over the roar of her racing pulse. She stepped toward the man, slowly. Gun out. Pointed at the body.

As she neared, she caught the slightest rise of his chest. He was alive.

Not murder, then. Attempted murder? Assault?

His face was swollen. He'd taken several blows in addition to the gash on his temple that bled profusely. She dropped to her knees at his side. She had no choice but to holster the pistol to check his vital signs.

His pulse was solid even though his breathing was shallow. It was likely a blessing that he was unconscious, because if he were awake she'd bet his head would hurt like a sonofabitch.

What to do? Whoever had done this to him could return. But if she left him here, unconscious, vulnerable, he could die. No. *Would* die. There were too many scavengers and predators in the area to believe he could survive, bleeding, unconscious, and alone.

But then, he could be the villain in this. Drug dealer. Poacher. Criminal on the run. This could be his just reward. She searched his pockets for a wallet with ID, but came up empty. His clothing didn't argue for poacher. His clothing—business casual slacks and a blood-saturated button-down shirt—didn't belong in these woods at all.

She checked his mouth, looking for rotting teeth, signs of drug use, anything that would indicate she had something to fear from helping him. But his teeth's perfect alignment could only be attributed to orthodontia. Bright white and nary a silver filling.

She opened his shirt, searching for other causes for his blood-soaked clothing besides the gash on his temple. All she found was hard muscle. Whoever this man was, he took good care of himself.

Given his build, in spite of his city clothes, he could be a Raptor operative who'd strayed from the compound. That thought had her considering leaving him. The bears and wolves could have him. Or whoever had done this to him could come back and finish the job.

She shook her head, knowing her thoughts were unfair. Not all the operatives on the Raptor compound were rotten. She got along with most of them and was even drinking buddies with Nicole. But she knew without a doubt a few operatives were up to no good, and she had a serious problem with their boss. But then, it was hard to have kind feelings for the person who might have covered up her brother's murder, especially when yesterday would have been that brother's thirty-fourth birthday.

She had to assume, given this guy's condition, he could be one of the operatives involved in dirty deals. The fact that she didn't recognize him only made him more suspicious.

She stood and slowly turned in a circle, scanning the woods. What should she do?

It was a five-mile hike—at least half of that uphill—to her truck. No way could she carry an unconscious man that far. Hell, there was no way she could carry him thirty feet.

She pulled out her first aid kit and dropped to his side again. She'd tend the head wound while she decided what to do. Using precious water from her water bottle, she dampened a pack towel and cleaned the gash on his temple. Given the blood, bruises, and welts, she'd have trouble recognizing him even if he were a regular at the Roadhouse, but she was fairly certain she'd never seen him in town, nor was he one of the operatives she'd met when she'd interrupted the live-fire training exercise and been arrested.

Her hands shook as she cleaned the gash, and she paused to steady her breathing and get the trembling under control. She scanned the woods, wondering if this man's attackers lurked nearby. Every instinct said to flee, but she couldn't abandon him.

He couldn't be a soldier attending a Raptor training, because after months of effort, she'd successfully gotten the government to shut down the compound's military training program while they investigated the company's safety measures. The weekly influx of soldiers had halted two months ago. But still, to be certain, she checked for dog tags and confirmed he wasn't wearing any.

Breathing under control, she swabbed his cut with alcohol again and applied antibiotic ointment. She closed the gash with three butterfly bandages.

Unless he had internal injuries she wasn't aware of, he'd probably be okay—as long as he wasn't left to die unconscious and alone.

She considered her options. She had plenty of parachute cord and a small but sturdy tarp in her backpack. With long, strong branches, she could build a travois-type stretcher and drag him to shelter.

But still…five-miles, much of it uphill. She closed her eyes, thinking of the surrounding area. After surveying this parcel of woods for the last four days, she knew this section of forest. Where could she take him?

There were a few very old caches, but she could no more haul him up into a cache than drag him five miles to her truck. However…Raptor land abutted the state forest about a half mile away.

She pulled out her USGS quadrangle map of the survey area and studied it. She'd checked the state database for historic and prehistoric sites on Raptor land as part of her search for Vincent's cave and had recorded all known sites—of which there were pathetic few—on her field maps, including this quad.

According to her map, there was a 1906 settler's cabin about a mile away.

She'd never been to that part of the compound; the closest she'd come was about a mile west. She couldn't be certain the cabin was still there, but she'd managed to find a few previously recorded sites in the parts of the compound she had explored, giving her hope that the historic cabin would also be extant.

After the live-fire training incident, the company CEO, Alec Ravissant, had acquired a restraining order to prevent her from stepping on Raptor land. But surely she wouldn't get in trouble for bringing an injured Raptor operative to the cabin, especially if the action saved his life? Of course, she couldn't admit how she knew the cabin existed, but she'd deal with that little problem if the time came.

But what if this man's attackers were in the cabin?

She didn't really have a choice. The cabin was his best hope. There was no cell coverage out here, and satellite phones were so horrifically expensive, she couldn't afford one. The hike to her truck plus the drive to where she could get a signal would take more than two hours. Help, in the form of emergency responders, would take another two hours to return. She had a feeling this guy didn't have that sort of time. Especially given his head wound and the evening wind, which was just beginning to kick up.

She dropped her hand to the gun at her hip. If there were men in the cabin, she wouldn't be helpless.

Before she could drag him a mile, she needed a travois. She set to work building it. Because she had a tarp, she didn't need most of the crosspieces; she could get by with one near the top and one at the bottom.

First, she used her knife to strip two six-foot-long branches, then she rolled the prepared branches into the opposite sides of the tarp at an angle, so it flared out, making it wider at the bottom, like a traditional travois. With the parachute cord, she lashed a short crosspiece to the top and a much longer one at the bottom, stretching the tarp tight in both places. The process took far too long for her peace of mind, but in the end she'd created something between a travois and a litter and could only pray the contraption would work.

She muttered an apology to the unconscious man as she rolled him onto the makeshift stretcher and strapped him between the poles using more rope, running it under his arms and over his shoulders. It would pinch and probably hurt like hell, but it was better than being left for dead, so he'd have to forgive her.

The man didn't make a sound, which increased her anxiety over his condition. With one last check of his pulse—still strong, thank goodness—she picked up the end of the travois and dragged him the first few steps.

Holy hell, he was heavy. She adjusted her grip and pulled another few feet, then stopped. She'd positioned him too high on the tarp, forcing her to lift too much of his weight. The poles should act as sled runners of sorts, but couldn't at the current angle.

She set him down and adjusted his position, lowering him until his legs hung off the tarp and the travois only supported his head down to his hips. Good thing he was unconscious, because he was about to be dragged across a whole lot of rocky ground, with nothing but a pair of cotton slacks to protect his skin.

After a hundred yards, she hit a snag. His sleeve had caught on a root because his arms dragged on either side of the tarp. With a short piece of cord, she secured both hands to his hips, running the thin rope through his belt loops instead of winding it around the travois and potentially causing even more hitches.

She stopped to rest often and quickly ran out of water. At least she could refill her water bottle from a stream indicated on the map—*please let it still be running this late in the summer*—and she had plenty of purification tablets. The aching, miserable, difficult, one-mile trek took two hours, but at last she reached the small meadow and spotted the cabin twenty yards away.

She paused on the edge of the woods. She was an archaeologist, not a police officer or Raptor operative. How should she handle this? Scout the cabin first with her gun drawn? Or was she *more* likely to get shot if she crossed the meadow obviously carrying a gun?

She decided to leave the gun in her holster and walk up to the cabin casually—a curious trespasser, not a suspicious vigilante.

The cabin was empty, and, given her difficulty in opening the door on rusted hinges, it had been for some time. But still, it had a floor—even if wavy, uneven, and soft—and a roof. One window held intact glass, but the other was broken. The single room was completely bare except for a stone fireplace on the back wall, and the hearth appeared sound. If she needed to, she could build a fire.

Most important, a crystal-clear mountain stream flowed ten yards away.

Shelter and water would get her and the injured man through the coming cold night.

She always carried the ten essentials and then some in her pack, so she had emergency rations to see her through the next twenty-four hours. Of course, if the man woke and was hungry, she'd run out food much sooner. But then, if he woke, he could walk his own sorry ass out of the woods.

She settled him on the wooden floor in front of the hearth, still strapped to the travois, then went to the stream to refill her water bottle. She splashed the chilly water on her face, overheated from the exertion of dragging a two-hundred-plus-pound man nearly a mile across hilly terrain.

Her shoulders burned, her knees ached, and her head throbbed with dehydration. She dropped a purification tablet into her water bottle but only waited a minute of the required thirty for the purification to take effect. She'd take her chances.

The water was crisp, cold, and tasted like iodine, but it was still the most refreshing drink she'd had in forever.

It was now after eight, long past the time she should have called the office to let them know she completed her survey for the day. Would anyone notice she'd failed to call in? Would anyone in the DNR office care if they did notice?

She pulled out her phone and typed out a quick text message. It failed to send; not enough signal. She'd expected that but knew there were places on the compound where the signal was too weak for voice calls, but texts still went through. She believed Vincent's last text message had been sent from such a place. For that reason, she always sent herself a text when she managed to stray onto a new area of Raptor land.

A noise in the woods—a stick cracking as if it had been stepped on?—startled her. She set down her phone and reached for the bear spray.

What the hell was she doing? The wind was kicking up as evening settled in, and she was stuck in the woods in one of the most remote forests in the United States. Worse, she was trespassing on the primary training ground of a paramilitary mercenary organization—which happened to be the one place on earth she was forbidden by court order from entering—and she had an injured stranger to watch over. Her first aid skills were rudimentary at best, and she didn't even know if the man was worth saving.

She studied the woods beyond the stream. Porcupine, wolf, caribou, bear, or any of a dozen other animals could have caused the sound. But there was also the chance it was a human predator.

It was a few weeks before the fall equinox, so even though the sun would set in a few hours, it wouldn't get completely dark, which meant if she built a fire in the hearth—and a clogged chimney didn't smoke them out—the smoke would be visible to anyone searching the area.

Which meant she couldn't build a fire for warmth, no matter how cold it got.

She toyed with the idea of leaving the man here and going straight to her truck. By herself, she could make it in two and a half hours. Three at most.

Isabel tucked her water bottle into the side pocket of her pack and stood with the bear spray still in her hand. Her knees wobbled, weak from the exertion of dragging the man through the woods. No way could she hike another six miles tonight. She'd go back inside the cabin, get out of the chill wind, check on the man, and rest for a few hours. She needed sleep. When her brain was clear and her head didn't throb so much, she'd be able to figure out what to do.

IT HAD TAKEN all of Alec's will to feign unconsciousness when he first came to as he was being dragged across jagged ground. His head hurt like hell, and he couldn't open one eye.

Who was pulling him? Where were they taking him?

How had he gotten here to begin with?

He thought back, trying to remember. He wasn't in Maryland. He'd gone on a business trip. Not for the campaign. It was Raptor business.

Where?

Not Hawaii.

Alaska. Yeah. Alaska. He peeked through one slitted eye and glimpsed a blurry forest canopy.

Definitely Alaska.

The compound was set to reopen. Next week.

That's right, I'm here to oversee the first training.

How long had he been here?

One day.

Had he even gone to the compound yet?

He didn't remember being there. He'd had a meeting scheduled, a one-on-one with Nicole, followed by a meeting with Falcon Team.

He remembered arriving in Fairbanks and driving south. And…that was it. Nothing after that. One moment he was driving, the next he was here, being dragged through the woods, none too gently.

His captor stopped at several points, but he didn't dare open his good eye when he was lowered to the ground. His one advantage was the fact that his captor had no clue he was conscious. It slowly dawned on him that his abductor was a woman, identifying the grunts and groans and curses as she struggled to haul his dead weight as that of a woman's voice.

What the hell?

Why was a woman hauling him through the woods? Why had she attacked him to begin with?

How had she attacked him?

The throbbing in his head told him whatever she'd done, it had been effective.

Tied down and being dragged, this wasn't the time for him to make a move. He'd wait, bide his time. Strike when just the thought of moving didn't make him want to vomit.

At last she dropped him inside a small, ancient, rotting cabin, and stepped outside. Once he was certain he was alone, he gingerly moved his arms and legs. No problem there. He turned his head. The room swam and nausea rose, but he could do it.

He felt at the ropes. He was tied to a tarp on a tree-branch frame. Clever. But she'd made a mistake. His hands, while bound, weren't immobilized. It didn't take much effort for him to slide free of the binding at his belt and work the knots that secured him to the travois until he'd freed himself.

Slowly, he rose, his balance wobbly, like a damn newborn colt, but again, he could do it.

"You sonofabitch! You made me drag you a mile when you could walk the whole time?"

Dammit! He'd been so focused on getting upright, he hadn't heard her approach. His Ranger buddies would laugh their asses off over this fuckup.

To hell with the throbbing in his head. This wasn't a time to hesitate. This was a time to fight through the nausea and pain. He lunged for her, grabbing her by the throat.

It didn't matter that she was a woman. No room for mercy given what she'd done to him.

She screamed, but the sound cut off as his grip tightened.

Blinding pain seared his good eye. His lungs burned. Then she landed a blow to his nuts. He released her, falling backward, doubling over.

This time, he did vomit.

ABOUT THE AUTHOR

Four-time Golden Heart® finalist Rachel Grant worked for over a decade as a professional archaeologist and mines her experiences for storylines and settings, which are as diverse as excavating a cemetery underneath an historic art museum in San Francisco, survey and excavation of many prehistoric Native American sites in the Pacific Northwest, researching an historic concrete house in Virginia, and mapping a seventeenth century Spanish and Dutch fort on the island of Sint Maarten in the Netherlands Antilles.

She lives in the Pacific Northwest with her husband and children and can be found on the web at Rachel-Grant.net.

Made in the USA
Monee, IL
22 July 2024